MW01138294

THE WRONG DRIVE

A SUSPENSEFUL HOLIDAY ROMANCE

ANNIE WILD

CONTENT WARNING

This book contains heavy themes that some readers may find disturbing. Reader discretion is advised.

PLEASE NOTE triggers may be spoilers.

Warnings include but are not limited to: *explicit sex scenes, death of parents, death of siblings, war-related deaths, car accident, suicide ideation, graphic violence on page, kidnapping, murder (on the page), attempted murder, verbal abuse, combat PTSD, mental health disorders, and attempted suicide.*

To all of those who have struggled with their mental health, you are worthy and you are deserving of love.

YOU ARE NEVER ALONE

- *USA SUICIDE HOTLINE: 988*
- *VETERANS SUICIDE HOTLINE: 988, then Press 1*

CHAPTER 1

EMERSYN

THIRTY-TWO MINUTES TO THE CABIN.

The radio blares an indie alternative song in my truck, and I tap my fingers against the steering wheel as I take in the desolate highway and snowcapped mountains in the distance. I check the time, knowing there's a chance for heavy snow at some point today. So far, all there's been is light flurries. It's a good thing, considering my driving abilities in snow are questionable at best—and Adam didn't feel like he could wait for me.

But...this is where my boyfriend grew up, and empathy isn't exactly his strong suit. He can handle the weather, and therefore expects everyone else to do the same.

I frown slightly at the thought. Two weeks alone with him in the Colorado countryside is about to begin, all with the intent of *resetting* our relationship—or something. Things have been rocky at best, and Adam was intent upon spending the time alone, saying we could bypass the holiday stress.

On the upside, I might actually get a white Christmas for once, since Oklahoma rarely gifts us with those. As I come to an intersection, my GPS chimes, breaking my thoughts and directing me to take a right, heading further north.

My phone buzzes in the console, and the music pauses with the incoming call. I see my best friend's name, which is surprising. She should be at work right now.

"Hello?" I answer.

"Hey..." Catie's voice has a drawl to it that I don't like one bit. "Are you close?"

"Um, sort of. Thirty-ish minutes to go. Why? Is everything okay?" I glance up to the rearview mirror, seeing a truck a few miles behind me. It's almost eerie, but the terrain is a beautiful mixture of desert peaks and mountains in the distance of southwestern Colorado.

"It is, but...I think we should talk before you get to the family cabin." Something in Catie's voice causes my stomach to sink, and I brace myself for the news as flurries turn to flakes.

"What is it?" I ask, eyeing the wet spots on the windshield growing. I hit the wipers, my heart thudding uneasily with the prospect of driving into bad weather.

"I was talking to Aaron, and well, I know the expectations you have for this trip..." Catie's voice is suddenly very quiet, and I'm wondering what information she got from her husband—who also happens to be my boyfriend's older brother.

I blow out a huff of air, and a strand of my natural caramel colored hair tickles my nose. "He's not proposing, is he?" I brush it out of my face, my tone sarcastic. "Seriously though, I have zero expectations. It's fine."

"Oh, don't be like that, Em," Catie urges. "I know it's not fine. You don't have to pretend like it is. I know you were hoping for something to change, and from what Aaron said, I don't..." She pauses or a few beats and then sighs. "*Ugh*, Adam told him he doesn't think it's going anywhere, and this is just his last-ditch effort to show everyone he tried. I wasn't going to call, but—"

"So, three years, and it's *not* going anywhere?" I exasperate, shutting my eyes for a moment, just long enough to steady my pounding heart. I *knew* it. I *knew* this trip seemed out of left field, and here I was, assuming he was attempting to care. "He's planning on breaking up with me, isn't he?"

"He didn't say that *exactly*," Catie says, her tone rushed.

"Well, but it's not going anywhere," I snap, shaking my head as the tears well up in my eyes. "I just took two weeks off unpaid for this." I feel like *such* a freaking idiot right now. This whole thing was all for show—to convince the rest of the world it's *me* not him.

"You can still go and enjoy it..." Catie's voice takes on an air of false reassurance. "I mean, maybe it's exactly what the two of you need, you know? It's been a rocky year for y'all. Maybe it'll change his mind."

"Yeah, it's been rocky because *he* never wants to answer my questions about commitment, and I'm tired of it. I'm thirty-one, not twenty-one. I'm over the games of men who don't know what they want, and here he is, telling me this vacation—which is causing me to miss out on time with my own family—is to help us reset. Really, he just wants the world to think he's the good guy before it's over for good."

"So tell him that?" Catie sighs, sounding borderline annoyed. "You can't keep venting to me, and never telling Adam this stuff."

"Right," I mutter, rolling my eyes. She's always trying to play neutral, given that she's married into his family. "I'll let you know how that goes." My GPS chimes at me suddenly to turn, and I slam on the brakes, almost missing my left-hand turn. *Shit.* The truck behind me blares their horn, and I cringe, shaking my head at my inattention.

"He was drinking when he told Aaron," Catie continues. "There's a chance that it's just more drunk Adam rambling. You know how he gets on the guys' night out."

"Yeah, maybe," I say. "I shouldn't have agreed to come on this trip, and I definitely shouldn't have assumed it might make things better."

"Don't beat yourself up, Em. I didn't know about it until Aaron met me for lunch today—and you're my *best friend*. Which is why I'm telling you to think about yourself for once. You deserve better, and maybe... Maybe you should call off the trip."

"So, you're saying *I* should break up with him?" I laugh dryly. "I just drove twelve freaking hours straight to get here. You don't think you could've told me this earlier?"

"I just found out," she pleads. "I'm sorry, Em. I really am."

I run my hand over my face. "It's fine. It's not your fault. The signs were there. I know that. It's not like I've been all that great of a girlfriend either. I always have one foot out the door anymore. I'm over it." *Lies. I'm not entirely over it.* A tear slips down my cheek as my vision grows blurry with more moisture.

Ugh. Using the sleeve of my sweater, I swipe at my eyes, smearing my mascara. The sick feeling of heartbreak is already slipping into my gut, and now I have to spend two weeks with a man who only cares about his *image* and not our three-year relationship.

"Maybe just talk to him," Catie says softly, probably hearing my sniffling now. "And then just come home. You can spend the holiday with us if you don't want to face your family right now."

"Yeah, okay," I mumble, turning down a gravel road.

The destination will be on the right in twelve miles.

"I'm almost there though. I'll let you go." I sniffle again, and then clear my throat as Catie and I hang up. It won't do my any good to be upset when I arrive—even if I'd love to crash my truck right into the side of his family's fancy getaway cabin.

The radio continues to blare, and I reach forward and punch the knob, turning it off. I'm not in the mood to hear anything anymore. I focus instead on the winding road, knowing good and well I'd be lost if it weren't for Apple Maps. I'm tempted to pick up the phone and call Adam, confronting him right now about everything, but God knows what that might lead to—and there *is* supposed to be snow moving in.

I need to just get there first.

I force long, deep breaths for the next ten minutes, and as I come to an intersection, I stop, taking in the desolation once again. I'm used to the middle of nowhere, but this is unfamiliar territory, and uneasiness slips up on me as the snow swirls around my truck.

It'll be fine. I'll just leave when the weather clears.

Unless he apologizes? Maybe Aaron got it wrong?

I let that thought run around my mind, just long enough for me to realize that the GPS is still stuck on the twelve miles to go.

Oh shit.

I furrow my brow at the screen, sweeping up my phone and checking service. It's minimal, but I do have a bar. Biting down on the inside of my cheek, I unplug my phone from CarPlay and pull over to the side of the road. I fumble with it, exiting out of the directions and trying to reload them.

"What the hell," I grumble under my breath as my phone screen freezes—and then won't reload anything at all. I glance up, and as I do, my heart does a flipflop in my chest. It's *really* coming now, and the visibility is suddenly minimal at best. I flip on my wipers as I try once more with my phone, growing more desperate.

Come on. I don't want to have to call Adam.

But with my attempts working to no avail, I pull up my boyfriend's phone number. I hit the call button and prepare myself for what's to come.

"Hey babe, are you almost here?" His tone is painfully jovial, and I wish I could reach through the phone and punch him right in the freaking face.

"Yeah, I was—I *am*," I say, staving off the emotions with my current predicament. "I'm only like fifteen minutes away, but my GPS isn't working for whatever reason."

He chuckles. "Not surprised. The service is hit and miss out here. Where are you?"

"Uh, great question," I sigh, pushing my hair out of my face again. "I made a turn onto a gravel road, and then it said I had twelve miles to go—I didn't get the road name or anything."

"Okay, so just clock it on your mileage. The gate is on the right-hand side of the road, and I think I left it open since it's snowing. But you need to hurry. The weather is going to shit —and quick."

I shift my half-ton truck into drive again and continue onward, grimacing as I break the news. "I'm honestly not sure how far past that point I've gone. I don't know if I can rely on the mileage."

He groans. "So you have no idea at all? What's the last road you passed?"

I cringe. "...I don't know."

"Figures. So... Um, well," he pauses. "If you're on the county road, you should just continue west. Maybe start counting your miles now. The layout is kind of weird out here. There's not a road every mile. When you get to the next intersection, tell me the road number, and I can help you get here."

"Okay. It's really snowing," I say, biting down on my lip nervously as the wind whips around my truck.

"You'll be fine," he grunts with little empathy. "Worst case scenario put it in four-wheel drive and keep going. You're close enough to make it."

"Yeah." I swallow the nerves pummeling me as the weather seemingly worsens with every passing second. I drive at a steady speed, ignoring the unnerving crunch of the snow under my tires. I can drive in mud or a downpour of rain, but snow and ice are not my forte. I'm from Oklahoma for heaven's sake. It doesn't snow all that much, and when it does... I just stay the heck home.

"Have you passed anymore roads?" Adam's voice chimes in my ear.

"No," I answer him flatly. "Though, I'm not sure I could even read the sign if I did."

"You're going to have to try and read it, Em."

"I know," I snap back at him. "I will."

"You'll be fine," he hums with an air of annoyance. "Just keep driving and take a few deep breaths. It's going to take a little bit for the roads to get unmanageable, and I have plenty of supplies here for us to wait out the blizzard."

"Blizzard?" I echo him, surprised. "I thought you said it was just supposed to just snow."

"Yeah, it's Colorado, honey. Just drive."

Keeping Adam on the line, I grit my teeth as press down on the accelerator. As I do, the back end of the truck spins out, and my heart jumps to my throat. *Slow and steady wins the race.* My palms begin to sweat, and I reach forward and turn down the heat in the cab.

At least the crappy weather is a distraction from the conversation we're going to have when I get there.

"See anything?" he asks again.

I squint into the snow. "Um, it looks like..." I catch sight of what looks like a side road off to my left, but it's nearly impossible to read the sign. Still, I squint, attempting to read the blur. "Ugh... Thirty-six, maybe?"

He's silent for a second. "Hang on."

I swallow hard. "Please tell me you know where I am."

He huffs. "Of course, I do. I'm just figuring how much further you have to go. I don't usually come in that way. I take the highway all the way to the turn off."

"Why did my GPS bring me this way?" I think aloud, my voice tinged with my inner panic.

"It's probably shorter, but the road sucks through there. It's fine though, you only have about a mile and half to go. Start paying attention to the dash."

"Right," I glance down and then reset my trip to make sure I don't miscount. "Got it. What's the entrance look like again?"

"Black gate on the right side of the road. You can't see the cabin from the road or entrance. It's a fairly long drive, but you should be able to make it. If not, I'll come get you."

"Yeah, I should've left earlier," I mutter as I watch the tenths of a mile tick by. "I should've just have come with you."

"You're the one who had the writing workshop, Em."

I roll my eyes. "And you're the one who wouldn't wait for me."

"Really?" he spouts off in a condescending tone, one that's become a regular occurrence. "I told you I'd wait, and you said not to worry about it. I can't read your fucking mind. I don't have superpowers."

"Yeah, sorry." I swallow the hurt and notice as my trip hits 1.2 miles. "I should be getting close."

"Great."

I take a deep breath, and to my right, I see an entrance with a large black metal gate—but my heart sinks. "I thought you said the gate was open."

He's silent. "Is it a black gate?"

"Yeah, surrounded by trees," I note through the whipping snow.

He sighs. "I may have shut it last night when I got in. It's just out of habit. My parents don't like it left open. You never know who might drive up. The isolation out here attracts strange people sometimes."

My shoulders slump as I slow down and turn into the entrance. "I'll open it then." Snow is already creating drifts and I grab my parka from the passenger seat, psyching myself up for the brutal cold. I wriggle into it and leave the phone on the console as I sling the door open.

The wind slaps me across the face as it catches my door. "Holy crap," I groan, forcing it closed before trudging to the gate. With freezing hands, I fumble with the dummy locked lock. I unwrap the chain, hanging it off to the side. I slide the bolt style bar, and push against the metal pickets to swing the gate inward. It gives with a wretched squeal, and I shove it open enough for my truck to fit through.

My feet are already freezing, and the bottom of my jeans are wet from the snow. I jog back to my truck and climb in, shaking off the cold. *Forget this. Maybe I* don't *like the snow.*

I smash the gas as I pick up the phone. "I'll be there in a second."

"Sorry I didn't open it. But I swore it was open." His tone actually contains some remorse, and while it's not a lot, it brings a little relief.

"It's okay," I say, once again putting the truck in park once I clear the gate. "Do you want me to shut and lock it?"

"Yeah, if you can. Like I said, you never know who might show up. Better to make it harder for someone to get in."

"Yeah, I'm locking it," I mutter, my mind humming with a repeat of all the true crime documentaries I've watched. I climb out once again into the elements, bracing against the wind. I shut the gate and then click the master lock shut all the way, no longer leaving it dummy locked. I return to the truck and pick the phone up as I shut the door. "Okay, well the chain is locked now."

"Wait, what?"

"What?" I repeat it back to him, confused. "You just said to lock it, right? You never know who might show up...?"

"Honey..." Adam's voice trails off in a way that makes me instantly nervous. "There's no chain lock on the gate—just a slide on the inside. The Master Lock broke the last time my parents were here, and they just haven't relaced it."

I pause. "So... There's not a Master Lock with a chain?"

"No..."

"So then what the fuck did I just do?" I exasperate. "I just *locked* myself in—wherever the hell I am."

"Share your location with me," Adam's voice picks up a concerned tone. "I need to see where you are. I know most of the people around here...But there's no one close to us with a black gate. You had to have gotten turned around or something. Maybe you entered the address wrong."

My heart jumps with panic as the wind howls around the truck, rocking it. I reach for my phone and try to share my location with Adam, but the screen freezes. "It's not working."

"It's probably the weather," Adam says, his voice still calm. "Just drive up and tell them you got turned around. I can meet you there—wherever you are."

I have no idea if anyone is even going to *be* there when I pull up. I don't even know if this *is* a house. "I might as well just go home," I blurt out as I squeeze my eyes shut, fear thrumming through my body.

"What the hell is that supposed to mean?" Adam snaps. "Why would you leave? We've had this planned since summer, and for the record, you'd never make it out of here with the blizzard coming in."

"Catie told me what you told Aaron," I throw it out there, irritation, hurt, and frustration beating in my chest as I smash the gas and start the slight ascent into the trees.

"What are you talking about?"

"He said you told him this isn't going anywhere—and that this whole two-week holiday alone is for everyone to *think* you're trying to make things work with me." I want to rip my hair out, knowing this is a *terrible* time to do this. *I should've stayed quiet.*

Because Adam sure as hell is.

I glance in the rearview as the lump grows in my throat. I can't see the gate anymore, and I feel like I've been swallowed by the trees. My front tires bust through drifts as I continue, and as I careen forward, I finally spin out.

"I guess you're not going to say anything to that," I mutter, as I shift into four-wheel drive. "Cool."

"There's no point being like that," Adam hits back. "I was drunk, and things have been a wreck between us. I *am* trying. You can't listen to anything my brother says."

"Yeah, well, maybe it's time to just throw the towel in," I huff, rolling my eyes. *God forbid he* ever *be the problem.*

"Great. Whatever. Just call me when you know wherever the fuck you are. As soon as this shit clears, we'll go our separate ways. Isn't that what you want, Em?" I can hear the hurt in his voice as he hangs up the phone, and I toss it into the passenger seat...

Right as my truck gets stuck.

Chapter 2

Emersyn

You have to be kidding me. I throw it into reverse, my anger causing a lead foot against the gas. It jerks backwards, and then hangs again, the tires spinning. I put it back in drive and try to send it forward, but I only bury it further in the drift of powdery snow.

I glance around, my heart throbbing in my temple. "Fuck!" I shout at the steering wheel, punching it with the bottom of my fist. I push my hair out of my face, and then force myself to take a deep breath. I squint into the whirling of vicious white flakes, making out what I *think* might be a cabin about two hundred yards ahead. It's impossible to tell for sure.

For all I know, it might just be an optical illusion. I sweep up my phone and call Adam once again as I cut the engine and shove the door open. *Please answer.*

"I'm getting around to come and get you, even if you

want a break," he snaps with greeting. "I'm just waiting on you to tell me where the hell you are."

"I'm just calling to tell you I'm stuck," I say, the wind feeling like a blade on my face as I ignore everything he just spat at me. "And I guess I have to walk the rest of the way to the cabin."

He's silent.

"Adam?"

"You're kind of breaking up with the wind." His annoyed tone lightens. "Did you say you're stuck and walking now?"

"Yeah." As my answer leaves my lips, I hear something in the distance—something that sounds a lot like dogs barking. It sends a shockwave of nerves through my shivering body... *But at least it's a sign of life up ahead?*

"You said you can see the house, right?"

"I don't know..." I squint into the snow as I start forward, cradling the phone against my ear. "I think so." I make out some sort of structure, but it's almost impossible to tell for sure. "I hear dogs barking though."

"That's a good sign," he sighs, sounding relieved to some degree. "Just tell them you're stuck. Like I said, I can come and get you if you hurry up and get an address. I still can't see your location, Em. I'm already getting ready to leave. Most people around here are nice, and they're going to be understanding with the weather. They might be able to get you unstuck...again, *if* you hurry."

"I'm moving as fast as I can," I exasperate, my hiking

boots not warm enough for this kind of trek. "I should've put on my insulated boots."

"Just keep your head down, and you'll be—"

"What?"

Silence.

I pull the phone away from my ear, the sound of the dog's bark growing as the wind dies down for a moment. I look ahead in the break, spotting the two-story log cabin ahead. It's not nearly as far as I thought, and based on my distance judging skills, it's only about a hundred yards away.

I sniff hard, my nose already beginning to run. *I can make it.* I glance down at the phone, and see the *call failed* pop up on the screen. I let out a sigh as chills run down my spine. I'm alone in this, but it'll be fine.

Most people are nice. And hopefully these people are the nice kind.

But the thought is hardly comforting as all the reruns of crime shows start playing in my head. My hands shake as I break through the trees, and I hold onto my hood as the wind tries to tear it off. I have no idea what I'm walking into, and as the dog barking grows increasing incessant, I start to grow wearier.

I manage to make it another fifty yards before I can actually make out more details the cabin. It's not in the best shape, but it's not run down and abandoned, either. There's a dog baying, though I can't pinpoint from where, exactly.

Someone has to be home. They have to feed their dog, right?

With one hand holding my hood, I shield my eyes with

the other, and as I do, I think I make out movement on the porch. It's impossible to see all that well, but for the sake of how cold I am, and how desperate I am to get out of here...

"Hey!" I shout above the blowing snow. "I'm stuck, can you help me?"

There's no response. Maybe they can't hear me over the shrill of the wind. Or maybe it was just the dog? I yell out again, my voice cracking with the ache of the brutal cold in my lungs. It was in the fifties back home—which is where I should've stayed.

No one answers again, and as my eyes water, I do my best to blink it away. The snow doesn't seem to be coming down as hard at the moment. I sigh in relief, rehearsing what I'll say when I reach the porch.

I made a wrong turn, I'm really sorry. Can you help me get unstuck? My boyfriend is on the way. Or is it my ex-boyfriend? Are we even together anymore?

My mind comes to a screeching halt as a loud crack pierces the winter air.

And pain *sears* through my hand.

I drop my gaze down, seeing my shattered phone...*and blood.* A lot of blood. Holy shit. Did I... Did I just... Did I just get *shot?* The wind tears my hood from my head, and I drop the phone into the snow, droplets of crimson staining the white powder as I do. I blink back tears and charge into the trees, cradling my hand as I try to get a grip.

What the hell just happened?

I try to catch my breath as I lean against the tree, my back to the cabin. I turned down the wrong drive, obviously. Obviously, these aren't the *mostly nice* people I was hoping for. But still, this has to be a misunderstanding. I'm from Oklahoma. I get the trespasser thing, I do. I get backwoods vigilantes. But seriously, I mean no harm. I'm *just* stuck. I don't want to hang out here. I don't want to steal their shit and sell it for meth.

My eyes drop once again to my bleeding hand, seeing the bullet grazed the inside of my palm. I can't tell how bad it is right now—and I don't have time to worry about it. I tuck it up under the bottom of my black coat and squeeze, trying to stop the bleeding and calm my nerves.

Maybe it was an accident. Maybe it was just meant to scare me.

But those thoughts don't calm the terror pulsing through my veins. I could easily die out here. If the asshole that shot at me doesn't finish the job, the elements will. My phone is ruined, too. I take a deep breath, gathering the courage to peer around the tree in the direction of the cabin. Finally, I spot someone, and while I can't make out the details, I *can* see the rifle in his hands...*and* a massive dog lunging at the end of a leash.

I swallow hard. *Definitely not a nice person.*

His white camouflage parka hood and black neck warmer hide his face, and even through the snow, I can tell he's a big guy. Teeth chattering as the wind whips through the trees, I wrap my arms around myself, trying to ignore the red liquid staining the snow around my legs. I have to be standing in at least six to eight inches of snow—and it's only going to increase.

I glance back to the porch, where the man still stands, appearing to be scanning the area. My legs feel weak and numb beneath my dark jeans. My hand burns, and I try to think through what I should do. Do I call out again? Do I try to run back to the gate or my truck? Tears slide down my face as I tip my head back, closing my eyes.

Ugh. What do I do?

The dog bays again, the sound now more terrifying than before. I try to breathe, feeling frozen in place. I *have* to come up with a plan, *pronto.* I've never been so torn in my entire life, and as I lean to look again, I hope I'm not making a stupid mistake.

"My truck is stuck," I shout again, pleading with him as his head jerks in my direction. A shudder rolls down my spine as the black and tan dog on the porch responds with an even more urgent bay in *my* direction. "I just made a wrong turn, please help me."

I sound so fucking stupid.

But still, I wait for the man's response, and hold my breath as he tucks the rifle under his arm. My gaze follows him as he leans over...

And unsnaps the leash from the dog's collar.

You have to be kidding me.

A high-pitched whistle follows the wind, and I realize just how bad this is about to be as the dog bounds down the porch steps and into the snow. Will the dog attack? Or just find me? My eyes drift down to the snow, fresh blood smattered across it. A rumble of thunder jars me into motion, and I stumble away, deeper into the woods but in the direction of the road.

Please don't let me die today. Please.

CHAPTER 3

TURNER

ONE. Two. Three. Four.
I declare a cold war.

I pop my lips under my neck warmer, sweat coating them already. I sing my little chant in my head as I let Gunner loose to trail the trespasser. She's not armed from what I can tell, but she is bleeding from my first shot. She should be easy to track, and well, my Bloodhound needs the exercise before he's stuck inside. I could use some, too.

I keep a tight grip around my rifle as my boots thud in the snow. It's a poor time to go hunting, and I know it won't be long before she's frozen to death anyway. I *could* let her succumb to the elements, and then play a game of finding the dead body.

But that's not nearly as exhilarating.

"Where is she?" I ask Gunner as he trails out ahead of me. The wind covers her tracks, and the snowfall has picked up again. I still see tinges of crimson painted in the snow though. A wave of anticipation floods my system, and I grin beneath my face warmer. I don't know what will happen when I find her, but fuck knows, I needed to have a little excitement in my life.

I catch sight of movement in my peripheral, and instinctively raise my rifle, placing my finger on the trigger.

"Not yet. Not yet, Martin," I command myself under my breath. "Feel it out. Analyze the threat first."

But who cares? She trespassed. I don't need to analyze shit.

I frown as my hands begin to sweat beneath my gloves. I'm torn between hitting the high of watching her body drop in the snow, and investigating further, figuring out why some little brunette is running in my woods. I couldn't hear what she was shouting at me, and I have to admit, I'd like clarification.

Gunner lets out a warning bark, grabbing my attention. He's closing in on her.

Damn the luck. She's not moving quickly enough to give him a good chase. Maybe it's because she's injured and in possible shock? I knew I'd graze her when I took the shot, but I wouldn't think it'd slow her down too much. She should have adrenaline coursing through her veins right now. My mind flashes back to the phone dropping in the snow. I'll need to find that when the weather clears.

But damn, I hate phones. They bring trouble and it means *anyone* can find you. I don't like that. They're an invasive technological leech on society. She'd be smart to figure that out. As I continue on, I catch sight of a silver Ford F150. It's definitely stuck, buried in the snow and mud up to the middle of the tires. If it had been colder before the storm blew in, she probably wouldn't have gotten so buried. I chuckle.

Bad luck for her.

Good luck for me.

Quickly, I check the doors and see they're unlocked. I know Gunner will keep pressure on her, giving me a chance to check this out. I rip the door open and spot the bags in the backseat. Looks like she's going somewhere.

Home for the holidays?

My stomach rolls. *Fuck that.* I slam the door shut and hear a yelp somewhere out in the woods. I grunt out a low laugh, wondering if she mistook it for more gunfire. Lucky for her, I don't waste ammo. Not usually, anyway.

Sometimes, I can't stop once I start.

I make my way to the back of the truck, my rifle still in a ready position. I check the license plate. *Oklahoma.* "You're a long way from home," I say under my breath. More thunder cracks overhead, and I know I should be checking the weather radio. When I went into town for supplies, they said we might get snowed in for a few weeks. That didn't matter to me. I only go to town once a month, if I have to. I can't handle the crowds.

Actually, I can't handle *anyone.*

Gunner's bark cuts through the howling winds, and this time, it's choppier, letting me know he's waiting for me. Target has been cornered.

I raise my rifle in the direction and stealthily cross the terrain, my boots crunching quietly in the snow. I'm covered by the wind. It's blowing north, northeast, gusting up to fifty miles per hour. She won't hear me as long as I continue the way I'm going.

And then what do I do?

My lip twitches as I conjure up possible scenarios. I could shoot upon arrival, or I guess I could interrogate, have a little fun... I follow the sound of Gunner's bays, keeping my wits about me for the moment. *Or maybe I should just let her go?* I mull it over, knowing the odds aren't in her favor.

No one's ever made it out of here alive.

My muscles tense as I catch sight of Gunner, his body mirroring that of my own. He understands the drill of a good hunt, and his excitement drums up mine. I skirt along the trees, unbothered as the weather continues to worsen. My eyes lock onto my target, and I'm unsurprised by her lack of winter clothing.

She's from the south, after all.

Her green eyes widen as she spots me, her back up against one of the old pine trees. Her hand is still bleeding, and the sight makes me feel...*nothing*. "I...I..." Her voice is meek, fragile.

I glare at her, but I can't find the words as I take in the damp hair sticking to her face, the shitty cheap coat, and her soaked denim. She won't last two hours out here.

I'll put her out of her misery.

I raise the rifle, and her teeth audibly chatter as she wraps her arms around herself. The absolute terror in her eyes suddenly help me find my voice. She's so fragile, I have to pry.

"Why are you here?" The gravel in my tone booms as my gaze bores into hers.

"I..." Her lips are tainted a light shade of blue. I was wrong. She might not last the hour. "I was trying to... I thought this was..."

"Speak in full sentences," I bark, taking a step toward her. She winces. My finger is on the trigger now, reminding me of my old nickname.

'Get 'em, Trigger.' I hear Bradford's voice in my head, his hand on my shoulder. Those were the good days. Before I broke. Before everything in my life went to hell in a hand basket.

"I was supposed to be staying with my boyfriend for the holidays at his c-c-cabin," she begins. "And my GPS went to shit. He said a black gate, and I thought this was it, and I got stuck. He said he'll pick me up if I tell him where I am."

Alarms sound in my head. "He's on his way *here?*"

She gets this confused look on her face. "I don't know."

I think back to the truck. It can't be seen from the road where it sits. "Does he have this location?"

"I don't know." She lets out a defeated sigh, and in the moment, a tear slips down her cheek. I'm not sure there's anything particularly special about her. I don't really care about her as anything other than a warm body. But I *do* care if I'm going to have more visitors.

So, I repeat myself. "*Does he know where you are?*"

She meets my gaze again, and immediately, I sense she's considering the idea of lying. And in her defense, the smart thing to do in this situation would be to lie. If someone knows where she is, that typically *would* increase her chance of surviving this situation.

But I'm physically capable of digging two graves—if I even bother with it.

"He doesn't know," I answer for her.

A tear slips down her cheek again. I recoil at the sight. She might be better off dead. I run my tongue over my bottom lip, as Gunner inches closer to her, his tail wagging with unease...or *something else?*

"No," I warn him, and he stops a foot or so from her.

"I'm really sorry for bothering you." Her voice breaks, and she looks away from me. "It's been such a shitty day. I can maybe try to get unstuck, if you'll just let me—"

I shake my head, cutting her off from speaking. *"No."*

"Okay, well..." She lets out a dry, bitter laugh. "Will you just *do* whatever you're going to? Because the way I see it, I'll either die by that .308 you have, or I'll die in the elements."

"So, you're not a total idiot," I mumble under my breath.

"What?" Her voice is abrasive to my ears. I don't like it. I don't think I like her.

My rifle is still pointed at her chest. I could just shut her up indefinitely, but something about her grinds my instincts to a halt. I know if I pull the trigger, I might spend days, if not weeks, unable to shake her cold, wounded expression. It's happened before.

I don't want it to happen again.

Fuck, what a dilemma.

She takes an audible breath, and then pushes off the tree. The movement has me in motion before I even realize what

I'm doing. She lets out a cry as she falls to the ground face first, the butt of my rifle sending her there.

Okay. Temporary fix for now.

I use my boot to roll her over, and now that she's unconscious, I *really* see her. She's at peace momentarily, and I'm sure if she knew who I was, she'd be wishing I'd extend that peace right into eternity.

"What should we do?" I turn to Gunner, who shivers at a blast of sharp wind. I feel nothing in the cold. I went numb a long, *long* time ago, and maybe a stronger man would've ended it before it ever went this far—but something keeps me here.

Maybe I just enjoy the misery.

A migraine thumps in my skull, and I sling my rifle back over my shoulder. Bending over, I scoop the woman into my arms. The closeness of her body is strangely warm against mine, even with the outerwear between us... But then again, maybe it's the fact I haven't had a living person this close to me in almost a decade.

I swallow the feelings that follow that reminder. I keep my chin up as I trudge through the deepening snow. I pushed it staying out here this long with her. If someone is really on their way, they won't make it.

But they might call in search and rescue. I'll have to keep an eye out.

As I carry her back toward the cabin, I glance over my shoulder. I've never had someone show up here searching for anyone. I'm so far off the beaten path, I rarely have trespassers.

"Come on, Gunner," I call back to my dog. "We need to get her settled and then we'll pay the truck one last visit." I have no idea what I'm supposed to do with her—or what *getting her settled* really means. I've never taken someone home before.

My eyes cast downward on her face again. She's kind of pretty. I don't know that I see people that way anymore, but she fits some sort of standard of beauty, I suppose. I can easily say that her only makeup is the mascara smeared across her cheeks. Her freckles add to her appeal, splattered across her skin like paint on canvas. I stare at her a few moments longer, zoning out on her soft features.

Maybe I just haven't held a woman in so long, I'm enthralled by the smallest details. However, there was a time in my life when I drank beer, slept around, laughed for the hell of it, and was...*normal*. Now, I'm forty years old.

And *definitely* not normal.

I kick open the door and enter my cabin, my escape from the real world. The fireplace is blazing, and I stomp the snow off my boots after shutting us all inside. I cross the hardwood floors to the couch and dump her off, taking her in once more.

Maybe I should tie her up? Or get her out of the wet clothes? I drop my neck warmer and rub the unruly stubble on my jaw as I contemplate for a few moments. No answer comes immediately, and so I spin on my heels to head back out into the blizzard to retrieve her things.

THIRTY MINUTES LATER, I drop her bags by the door, once again eyeing her on the couch. She's still out, and that's a little concerning. I brush it off though and lock up the front door. The elements are worsening, and if someone was out looking for her, I know they aren't now. It's too dangerous for search teams to dispatch, and they'd have to travel a hundred miles to even get here. This isn't a touristy area.

No one is coming for her. For now. There's a strange air of excitement with that conclusion, but I don't know why. I don't like people. They never last long around me, anyway—even if I want them to. I frown at that, and kick my boots off this time, leaving them by the door. Gunner is somewhere inside, probably snoozing in my room. I strip out of my parka and hang it on the rack by the door, and then slide out of my coveralls as well.

I'm left in my black sweatpants, henley, and wool socks as I creep across the floors to check on the woman invading my space. I clench my jaw as I take in the serene way she's laying there. I don't know if she's just that fucking tired, or if I knocked her out a little too hard. I have things I could give her to keep her out...

That would probably be for the best until I make up my mind.

I mean, I can't discern the severity of her concussion, and if she just doesn't wake up, well... That's out of my hands. She's the one who trespassed and got stuck. It's not like I baited her here or something. My gate was shut for fuck's sake.

And that might be why I've left her living. It's hard to say if it's a rare occurrence of sympathy or just some kind of sick intrigue.

My eyes glide down to her denim, and I stare at the dark, still soaked place around her upper thighs to her ankles. A twitch tugs at my upper lip, and I rake my fingers through my hair. I'm not sure why it seems like a mountain of a task, given the life I fully lived up till the age of twenty-nine. But it does.

I spin on my heels and head to the door where I dropped her things, quickly unzipping the top black duffle bag. Much to my relief, there's a pair of gray sweatpants on top. I pull them out, catching the hint of lavender detergent. I wince at the scent, my stomach furling. I hold them out and away from my body as I return to the woman.

I don't even know her name. But maybe it's better that way.

If I know her name, it might make it more scarring when she's a mound of dead flesh. A sick taste hangs in my mouth, and I shake my head. I don't have to think about that right now. I'm fine.

I'm fine. Everything is fine.

I toss the sweatpants on the arm of my faded leather couch, and then reach for her, my hands landing on her hips. The warmth of her body sears my calloused palms. *Fuck, it has been so long since I touched a woman.* Gritting my teeth, I roll her gently onto her back. A light moan slips from her lips, and a thrum of something old and familiar hits my groin.

Ah, good to know that part of me still functions.

Pushing it aside, I stick to the task at hand, removing her shoes and then unsnapping her jeans. As I tug them over her hips, I'm met with the sight of her skin, glistening under the glow of the fireplace. Freckles dot the pale skin in places, and I try to ignore the way her black satin underwear are like a magnet for my gaze. My knuckles brush her bare skin, and my heart throbs in my temple.

Could I make her feel good if she wanted me to? It would only be fair since I know her ending. Maybe it'd make it less painful if she had something pleasurable to go with it. I chuckle to myself, knowing good and well, I'd just scar her more. Or myself.

So, I push it away, pulling the jeans the rest of the way off her and tossing them toward the warm floor in front of the fire. I swallow the knot in my throat as see her stretched out in front of me. Primal urges tug at me.

But I don't listen. I have self-control. *In that way.*

I retrieve the sweats and work her into them, letting out a sigh of relief when she's fully covered again. I'm still a gentleman, despite being fucked in the head.

My monsters are of an entirely different kind.

CHAPTER 4

EMERSYN

WARM.

I feel *warm*. Not hot. Not cold. Just...warm. And for a moment—a very, *very* short one—I forget what happened to me. However, my throbbing hand is enough to bring the memories crashing down. My pulse picks up as my eyes flutter open, halfway expecting myself to be chained in a basement.

But I'm *not*.

My fingers brush the leather material beneath me, and I adjust my eyes to the living room, alight by the glow of a fireplace. It's...*cozy*. The flames cast an orange glow across a quaint sitting area, and while it's not Hallmark level of comfort, it's not roughing it, either. Off the living room, there's a kitchen, but I can't make out much. The wind howls outside, and as my eyes track back, a chill runs down my spine.

Somehow, in all my waking up, I missed the dark figure

sitting in the armchair across from me. My heart jumps to my throat as I take in the shadow of a man, his face partially illuminated by the fireplace. I can make out his strong set jaw, the slight dimple in his chin, and his dark, hooded eyes.

He's terrifying.

I rip my gaze from the shadow man to my hand, properly bandaged. That's when I notice my jeans have been replaced with sweatpants—that were in my luggage. My mouth runs dry at the realization that he *at a minimum* changed my pants. I press my hand against my forehead, just realizing I have a headache.

"It'll fade," the man grunts at me.

I don't say anything immediately, working my fingertips to the sore spot on the back of my head. There's a knot and while it's still painful to the touch, it's not *that* bad. I've had worse injuries, I guess. I press my hands back down against the couch, and slowly, rise to a sitting position, all while eyeing the man a few feet from me. His knuckles are white as he curls them into the leather. The motion causes lightheadedness as my blood pressure takes a drop.

"How long have I been out?" I ask, my voice cracking with every syllable.

It seems to grate his nerves as what little of his jaw I can see twitches. "Hours."

I narrow my gaze. "How many?"

"Enough for your head to feel better."

My mind can't wrap itself around his cryptic reply, and I don't even try to understand. I take a deep breath, expecting myself to feel panic, fear—something, but instead, I don't really feel anything at all. Other than confused.

Really freaking confused.

"I should probably call my boyfriend." I pause, my voice quiet. "Well, ex, I think," I add under my breath, the realization causing my chest to ache. I look up at him when he's still silent. "Can I use your phone?"

He's unmoving. "No."

"You *shot* mine," I exasperate, the volume of my voice scorching the quiet crackle of the fireplace. "He could be out in *that*." I gesture to the window. "He's probably worried."

The man's cold expression doesn't budge. "Okay."

My shoulders slump. "I *need* to let him know I'm okay. He'll probably call the cops, and—"

He shrugs. "They won't find you."

I blink a few times to clear the moisture brimming my eyes. "I don't understand. He's going to come looking for me."

"He'd be an idiot to try that in this storm. If there was a search, they've called it off by now." His voice is so monotone, it's creepy. "They'll wait until it passes."

"You don't know that," I say stupidly.

"Okay."

My heart hammers against my ribcage. *Who are you?* I want to shout at him, but his aura is intimidating—and almost as frightening as the charged silence in the room. My palms sweat and the warmth in here is now suffocating. I eye the door to my left.

"You'll succumb to the elements within an hour."

"You don't know that." I sound like a complete idiot as I repeat myself, and for the moment, I justify it with the hit on the back of my head. The man doesn't react to anything, continuing to sit there in the chair and assumingly stare at me. I shift uncomfortably.

"You should hydrate." He nods to the side table.

I follow his gaze to the bottle of water sitting there. It's open. "Can I have one that's still sealed?"

"You think I'm roofying you?"

I swallow hard. *Jeez, this man makes me nervous.* "I don't know you."

"I don't know you, either. I think it's fair to assume you're the one who trespassed onto *my* property. Therefore, *you* are more likely to be a threat."

I narrow my eyes. "You tried to shoot—"

"Just drink the fucking water," he barks at me.

I nod out of fear, trying to reason with myself. Maybe he's just an introvert and so he's cranky I'm here. I mean, anyone who lives in a cabin alone with their dog and shoots phones out of people's hands has to be recluse. *Or insane.* But maybe he's paranoid? Doom's day prepper. I cast my gaze over him again.

Maybe.

"You're a good shot," I think aloud, the mental image of my shattered phone coming back to mind. He could've easily misjudged with the wind and low visibility—and *killed* me. *Or maybe that's what he was trying to do.*

He doesn't say anything to my comment, and anxiety creeps into my chest. I've always been the annoying kind of person who talks to fill the space. I hate that quality about myself. I'd change it about me in a heartbeat.

But I'm also *so* freaking confused and terrified by this situation.

He shot my phone, his dog trailed me through the woods, and then he knocked me unconscious. I'm not bound and gagged... But there's also nowhere for me to go.

And what about my change of pants?

I push my hair out of my face and wrap my arms around myself. Never mind the breakup—er, break when it comes to Adam. This is much, *much* worse. I'm probably in a house of horrors, and this is just the beginning.

All I can do is hope like hell there's a search team out there coming for me. There's no way Adam would just let me *disappear* like this. My hands begin to tremble in my lap, and I swing my legs down, my feet hitting the cold hardwood floors. I shiver. All the while, the man's dark eyes just bore into me, gauging my every move.

"You changed my pants," I comment as I slowly go for the water, seeing his gaze follow my arm.

"Yeah."

"Why?" I pick up the bottle and unscrew the lid, nerves rolling through my stomach so hard, I begin to feel nauseous. *Did he do anything to me?* I shift uncomfortably. *I don't think so. I don't feel like I've been violated.*

"Your jeans were wet."

I study his face for a few moments but then nod, taking a sip of the water to avoid him noticing the heat flushing my cheeks. This man saw me partially unclothed. *Yikes.* I focus on my actions instead. I'll test the drink with just a little sip at a time, and if I start to feel off, I'll stop. Self-preservation, I guess. Though, I have to admit the moment he had me cornered, there was a part of me that wished he would've just pulled the trigger over dragging me into his cabin.

But maybe he's just a backwoods mountain man. That would literally be best case scenario at this point, but let's be honest, I'm just trying to make myself feel better. I'm probably going to die a horrible, painful death at the hands of this guy. My mind plays with that idea as I take another shaky sip. I'm so freaking thirsty, but so scared I'll pass out again.

He won't let me even use his phone.

I take a stab at him, trying to talk away my growing panic. "Why can't I use your phone to call someone?"

He shrugs, his thick shoulders bobbing only slightly. "Don't have one."

I furrow my brows, not for one second believing him. "You don't have a phone? Not even a landline?"

He just stares at me.

"Okay," I mutter, more to myself than anything. "Do you know how long this snow is going to last?"

"Couple of weeks."

"That's how long to expect to be snowed-in? Or how long the blizzard itself will last?" He chuckles, and my heart skips a few beats at the sound. "I'm from Oklahoma," I clarify. "We don't get snow like this."

"I know."

I clench my fists. "Okay, so then how long is the actual snowstorm going to last?"

"Three to four days."

I breathe a sigh of relief. "And then I'll be able to leave?"

"No."

My chest tightens. "Why?"

"By the time they get out here to clear the roads, the second storm will move in," he reasons, his tone bitter with annoyance.

The urge to cry bites at me, but I push it away. Losing it in the woods with this guy was embarrassing enough. "So, when will I be able to leave?"

"Stop asking so many goddamn questions," he roars, jarring me. I brace as he pushes himself to standing, his six-foot-something, muscular frame towering over me. I shrink away, preparing to be attacked, but he only shakes his head. "Just shut up and drink the water."

His boots thud across the floor, and my eyes follow him as he disappears down a dark hallway off the main room, leaving me alone. I wait for what feels like hours, though I know it's just minutes, expecting him to return... But he doesn't.

Where's the dog? I scan the room, and then carefully, stand to my feet. I set the water down, and ease across the living room, my socks silent. Clearly, my host is an abrasive asshole, and I think it's safe to assume he's dangerous.

And pissed I'm here.

I enter the kitchen, a dim light on above the stove. He still has electricity despite the storm, so that's a plus. A chill wafts through air and I shiver again, wishing I had a blanket or coat. I glance around and my eyes land on the fridge, my stomach growling. God knows how long it's been since I've eaten. I don't know the date. I don't know the time.

And it's sobering.

But surely, *someone* is looking for me, right? I mean, Adam? And what about my family and friends? They'd be unable to reach me? And I'd think Adam, despite us not being together or whatever, would tell them what's going on?

Ugh. The thought nearly sends me to my knees. I take a deep breath, and decide to keep creeping, focusing on the inherent risk I'm taking instead of everyone panicking over me going missing in a blizzard.

Making my way to the fridge, I continue to take in my surroundings. Paranoia and fear hang heavy over me, still unable to let go of the image of him coming after me with that rifle tucked in the crook of his shoulder—like he was going to use it. I shudder as I open the door.

It's stocked to the brim with nonperishables.

But as much as I want to take something out to eat, I know I shouldn't. I shouldn't touch anything. He might kill me. With that thought, I close the fridge and catch sight of a butcher block. Would it be stupid to take a knife and hide? Or would it make him more distrusting of me? I swallow hard as I contemplate the situation. Nothing could prepare me for this, and I know if this *is* a dangerous situation, my survival will require reading him correctly.

So, I leave the knives alone.

I retreat to the couch, my stomach sick and my heart aching. My mind replays the tense conversation I had with Adam before the call dropped. I hurt him. He hurt me.

Again. He said what he said to his brother, but he'd been right about how rocky we've been. We can't get along for whatever reason, and maybe it's because I feel so fucking *stuck* in life right now—like I'm getting nowhere at all at thirty-one.

And I hate it.

My job as a content writer is fine. It pays the bills, but just because the bills are paid, doesn't mean that I'm happy with it. I've been in the same place since I was twenty-seven, and the last four years just blew by. I thought Adam was the next step...

But he was just as stagnant, and when we started bickering, respect for each other flew out the window.

Or maybe he's always been that way? Am I just now seeing it?

I sigh, raking my fingers through my hair. I pull my knees into my chest, eying the pitch-black hallway that swallowed my host. I let myself stare at it for a few moments, and then allow myself the freedom to let the tears loose. I don't think he's coming back anytime soon, and that's about the only comfort I have for now.

So, here's to being trapped with a horrifying asshole, and praying my freshly ex-boyfriend will figure out how to rescue me before I die in this cabin.

CHAPTER 5

TURNER

SO MUCH FUCKING CRYING.

She thinks she's being quiet, muffling it with her head pressed against her knees, but it sounds like nails on a chalkboard to me. I hate it.

I hate her.

Well, I hate the way her cries tug on what little shred of humanity I have left, torturing me with the reminders that before I became *this,* I was human. Twenty years ago, I would've sat beside her and at least offered some semblance of comfort—maybe a hand on her shoulder? A hug? I don't know.

Regardless, back then, I sure as hell wouldn't be standing in the shadows of the hallway watching her like the freak I am now. I don't know how talk to her in a civilian way. I can't remember the last time I had an interaction that wasn't a 'thank you,' at the fucking store. I grind my teeth as I clench and unclench my fists.

Maybe I should've let her use my old, dead phone.

But honestly, I don't know if it even works anymore, and I *don't* need visitors of any capacity. I sigh quietly, and my gaze darts back to her on the couch.

The things I could do to silence her flick through my head, and none of them involve getting within a few feet of her. I clamp my lids together, drawing myself into the darkness, as the banging and screaming begin in my head again. A nudge from Gunner causes my eyes to flutter open, and I glance down to him sitting beside me. He's supposed to know when my demons come for me, and he does...

But he can't stop the worst of them anymore.

No one can.

She's not safe here with me.

When the urge to kill comes, I *kill.* There's no stopping me. Her sobbing for whatever reason is already pushing me toward losing it, too, and there's nowhere for her to go if I do. She'll never survive a blackout. My eyes flicker to the walls of the hallway, where pictures of my good memories once hung—before I ripped the mangled frames down. A sob tears through my psyche again.

FUCK. I have to stop her crying before these walls are smattered with her damn brains.

I crack my knuckles and slip out of the shadows. It's mid-afternoon of Saturday, December 14th, and it might as well be the middle of the night with the blizzard hanging out overhead.

Her cries instantly cease as the floor creaks. Her head jerks up at the sight of me, and the way her green eyes widen with fear only serves to remind me of who I am. I'm a nightmare. My home is the last place you want to end up stranded.

And I sometimes abhor myself for it. *Sometimes.*

"Are you hungry?" I grunt out, trying and failing to sound pleasant. Though, maybe if I feed her, she'll shut the fuck up.

"Um," she sniffles, her eyes red and puffy. "Yeah. I can make myself food. I don't want to be a burden."

"Impossible to prevent that."

She winces at my response, her eyes dropping to her hands. "Okay, well, I can do my best to be *less* of one."

"I don't like people touching my stuff."

"You have granola bars," she reasons, eyeing me. "I can just have one of those."

So she's been in my kitchen. Anger tugs at me, but I push it off. I can't decide if she's a manipulative brat, or if she's being sincere. "Okay," I finally say. I sidestep into the kitchen, keeping my eye on her as I open the pantry and grab two. She needs to eat and drink. Basic human needs.

Oh shit. She should also need a bathroom?

I blink twice at that as I return to the living room. There's only one bathroom in the cabin. It's through my room. I don't like that idea.

It won't last long. The moment she triggers me, or I get annoyed, she'll be dead. This courtesy won't last forever. I hold out the granola bars for her, and she's careful not to touch my hand, grabbing them by the very end. Her instincts must be kicking in, sending her signals that I'm a danger to wellbeing.

43

That won't save you, I want to tell her, warn her of what's coming. But then again, it might be better to bring her death without warning. I don't want to give her the false hope she'll survive me...

No one ever does.

"Thank you," her voice cuts through my thoughts. "Can I use your bathroom?"

Again. Basic human needs.

"Yeah, okay." My muscles tense as she stands to her feet. I take in the fragility of her, and the way she staggers when she takes a step.

Fuck, one hit and she'd be done... I could easily pummel this woman. She stands maybe five-feet-four. She's not skin and bones by any means, and while I think she's got some fight in her, she'd be no match for me. That's the difference between her and those before her. They were different—they were *challenges.* She's no fucking physical challenge, and it's got me hung up.

She clears her throat. "Where is it?" She smooths at her hair, though her brown locks are a matted mess. She needs a fucking shower. Would I have to sit in the bathroom to make sure she doesn't try anything? My body reacts to that thought, and I let out a grunt.

"Last door on the hallway, through the bedroom on the right. Your suitcase is over there." I nod to the bags by the front door. I went through her purse enough to know she's Emersyn Lewis. Thirty-one years old. Her current address is in Stillwater, Oklahoma. She's a writer of some sort.

Which confirms that she is, indeed, *weak.*

And once upon a time, I would've beat my chest that *I* was the fucking lunatic protecting people like her, Mr. Special Ops out to keep weak little writer girls safe. But now, I don't think so. She got herself stuck here. I owe her nothing.

"Is there a shower?"

Jeez. She asks the stupidest questions.

"Yeah," I say flatly. She watches me warily as she makes her way to her luggage, picking up her black duffle bag. My gaze drops to her sweatpants as she bends over. I changed her jeans in a haze of duty, but I still recall the way the glow of the fire lit up her bare legs as I did. I could've stared at her longer. I suddenly wish I would've.

My body reacts once more, and I watch her disappear down the hallway. *Fuck,* if I let her live, will I want to touch her? Get close? I know I probably won't. But there's this deep, buried part of me that *likes* the idea. I've been holed up here, living the cycle of my broken psyche for years. Maybe I *could* find some pleasure.

No, bad idea. My thoughts stand to reason with me. I don't know what would happen if I tried. And what if I got attached? I swallow that thought. There's no way I could let someone *know* me....

'You don't need to be alone,' My brother's voice in my head hits me right in the gut. *'I want better for you.'*

You had no fucking clue, Tommy. No clue.

My poor older brother thought I got an honorable discharge when I left the Marines. He had no idea that I snapped the way I did. And I only made it out uncuffed because Bradford, my commanding officer, had some sort of sick pity on me.

'Disappear, find some way to get your fix or get help, Martin,' I hear his words in my head. *'And if you choose the first, just don't fucking get caught.'*

And that small spew of words is what led me here. I nabbed my dead parents old hunting cabin and made it my fucking prison for life. As long as I stay here, no one gets hurt. Well, except for the fucking fools who have trespassed or tried to make friends.

I start down the hallway, hearing the pipes fill with water. I worked hard to make sure this cabin could make it through the bitter winter, and now someone else is experiencing the benefits. I'm a selfish asshole, but it's strangely satisfying for some reason.

Enjoy the hot water, I think as I hesitate outside of the bedroom door. I reach for the knob and turn it, opening the door in silence. I'm a fucking brute for infringing on her space like this, but also... This is *my* house.

I pad silently across the floor to the bathroom door. It's closed, but there's no lock on the door. My tongue darts across my bottom lip as I hear a hum on the other side of the door. She's *singing* to herself in there. I nearly laugh, though my dick seems to like the sound of her sweet alto voice carrying through the air.

It's the first time I've heard any semblance of music in years, and as I fight the urge to come unglued, I listen a little closer. I don't recognize whatever is coming out of her mouth—but that's not all that surprising. Again, I haven't listened to anything in almost a decade.

Finally, it hits as I process the lyrics. She's singing some sort of heartbreak song, and I curl my lip in disgust.

Probably her fucking boyfriend.

That *enrages* me. My fist collides with the door and it slams open, the knob going through the drywall. "Shut the fuck up," I growl at her.

She yelps, spinning around while trying to cover herself through the foggy glass. "I-I-I'm sorry."

I rake my gaze over what curves I can make out through the glass, suddenly turned on and pissed off, all at the same time. "I don't want to hear you sing," I say, sounding fucking psychotic—even to myself.

"Uh..." Her eyes hold mine, confusion and terror riddling them. "Okay. Okay, I won't. I'm sorry. I just didn't know."

Fuck. Me, either. What is wrong with me? The moment causes me pause, and I slip away, heading for the staircase to the lookout. I clearly don't remember how to blend in like I used to. I feel like the beast in the castle, only poor Belle won't get to kiss me and turn me into a prince.

No, no way in hell.

I thud up the stairs, taking the blind corner, inwardly bracing as per usual. I pass the first door. It's the room I don't enter. It's got nothing but reminders of who I once was. That's not me anymore. Well, maybe I've always been a psychopath, but that was back when I tried not to be. Maybe I just wore a mask and wore it well.

Hmm. Never considered that.

Regardless, now I know I'm a fucking menace to humankind. I'm the nightmare in people's dreams. I'm a hunter that only gets a high if the blood that spills is of a person with a soul. I don't care if it's your father, brother, son, or uncle. A grave is a grave, and I've got too many in my backyard.

I open up the door to my lookout, frowning at the window with no view due to the blinding snow. I pull out the chair at my desk and take a seat, letting my mind draw back. I started out trying to work out my problems like anyone else—a therapist, medication, whatever. Then one day, I had a hunter decide to trespass on my property. He started a fight, and I took my shot, adrenaline pulsing through my veins.

And it all went downhill from there.

I started actively waiting for people to trespass, their unwanted presence triggering my broken mind. Believe it or not, it happened more often than one would think, especially during hunting season. They weren't supposed to be here anyway, so when they got a bullet to the head, no one came here looking.

However, in a total of seven instances in the last decade, I've never had *this* happen. A woman has never graced this land since my mother, and Emersyn has something about her that makes my body remember its primal urges. I start to picture her bare legs again, the way her dark hair was matted to her head in the shower, and the curvature of her hips through the foggy glass.

I drum my fingers on the desk, as my dick grows hard. *Emersyn.* Before I realize what I'm doing, I unbutton my jeans and set my cock free. I start to stroke, and then think of her mentioning her boyfriend. I immediately grow limp.

No, I want to share her. I conjure up a scenario where she changes her mind, where fear turns to desire, and she *falls* for the beast.

I know that's bad, *bad* for me, but when I want something, I take it.

And I think I *want* Emersyn Lewis.

CHAPTER 6

EMERSYN

SOMETHING IS wrong with this man. Big wrong.

I have no idea who he is, but my instincts are screaming that I'm *not* safe here. Shivering from the cool draft of the open bathroom door, I step out of the shower and wrap my towel around myself. I don't know his name. I don't know if I even *want* to know his name.

I just want to get the fuck out of here.

But the winds continue to howl as I dry off and get dressed, pulling on a pair of jeans and a black sweater. I run a brush through my towel dried locks and ensure the rest of my makeup is gone from my face. I have no desire to *be* desirable to this man. I just want to be invisible. Maybe *that* is the ticket to making it out.

Maybe this is how Belle felt in the castle with the beast.

I purse my lips at the elementary analogy, and then hang the damp towel on the rack. I put all of my things back in my bag, ensuring that I leave nothing behind. Maybe he'll let me stay in a spare room...and then I'll never come out.

Nodding to myself at that scenario, I sling my bag over my shoulder and take a deep breath. Fear and apprehension pulse through my veins as I emerge from the bathroom, stepping into the dark bedroom. He's not there, and for some reason, that's all the more unnerving. I don't know what I'm supposed to do.

I just wish I wouldn't have come here at all. But there's no point in dwelling on the fucking past and my stupid decisions. I'd thought all this time that Adam and I's holiday getaway might be an actual fix. It was a joke, and really, maybe I knew it all along.

My bare feet creak across the floors as I start down the hallway. I squint in the dim light. My stomach lurches violently as I remember the man seeing me naked through the glass.

Would he hurt me? Well, I mean, beyond shooting my hand and knocking me unconscious.

A chill rolls down my spine, and I continue forward. Lingering in the hallway seems dangerous—like he might jump from the shadows and grab me. I step into the living room, passing what I assume is the back door. The glass is covered with a curtain. All the windows have large blackout curtains. *Maybe he's just paranoid. Or fucking psychotic.*

Yeah, I'm going with the latter.

"I'm making dinner." A voice startles me, and I jump sideways, slamming my shoulder into the wall. He doesn't react to my jerky movement, and his stone-cold demeanor is fucking terrifying.

"I have the granola bars." I nod to my bag. "I don't want to impose. Actually," I pause, meeting his deep, dark brown eyes. "I was thinking if you have a spare room, I can just stay there. You'll never know I'm here, then when things clear up, I'll be out of your hair. Give me a shovel and I'll dig my way out." I let out a stilted laugh, and he, once again, doesn't react in his facial expression.

"Mm," he grunts. "You can eat dinner."

I hesitate, tempted to repeat myself but hold off. "Okay. Can I put my things somewhere?"

He nods to the place by the door. "Back where I set them."

"But it's blocking the door," I reason. "I can put them in a spare—"

"I don't have a spare room for your use," he snaps, cutting me off. "Set the bag by the door." His harsh tone silences me, and I merely nod, ducking away and walking past him.

I set my duffle back on top of my hard suitcase and drop my shoulders as I push the bags against the outer wall. He's forcing me to be in his sight. All the fucking time. I glance back over my shoulder, noticing the kitchen light is on with a pan on the stove. It gives me a better view of him, and I see his muscular form clad in a worn out henley and black sweats. His physique is attractive, and his dark hair is clean cut, longer on the top with a fade. So, he might be psychotic, but at least he cuts his hair?

He turns to me, and I drop my gaze away. "I don't have a lot of variety."

I run my tongue over my bottom lip, forcing myself to meet his eyes. "That's okay," I say, assuming he's talking about food. His expression shifts slightly, and I catch my breath at the *almost* softness in his gaze. He appears embarrassed or...*guilty?*

Regardless, it draws out his handsome features. A strong nose and jawline. Deeper set eyes and dark brows. His hair has a tinge of gray, and I wonder how much older than me he is. Not *that* much. It's then I notice the ink, scrawled up to his chin. I hadn't seen it in the shadows. Depictions of violence are *everywhere* on his skin. I swallow hard, hating how it goes straight to my core.

"You can sit at the table while I finish," he gestures to a small round breakfast table tucked off the kitchen by windows with more curtains covering them. There are two chairs, and I opt for the one that faces him. I run my fingertips across the smooth dark grain as I try to keep my breaths steady, my heart racing. I'm going to give myself a fucking heart attack if I can't get control of it.

He returns to the stove and throws two steaks into the pan. He then grabs another pan and a sealed bag from the freezer. I watch him in the plain light, wondering how someone, who appears increasingly more handsome by the moment, could be so incredibly terrifying.

"You're from Oklahoma?" he asks, not looking at me as he speaks.

"Yeah," I answer him.

"Never been."

"Not missing much." I force a laugh, and he cocks his head in my direction. I instantly shut up, my eyes falling to my clasped hands.

"I'm from Utah originally."

I nod at the tidbit of information, stealing a glance back up at him. "Never been."

"Not missing much." His lip curls up slightly—he's *almost* smiling.

I can't help it. A real laugh slips through, and heat flushes my cheeks. My heart rate slows slightly, but the flutter in my stomach remains. The aroma of the steaks and vegetables fill the cabin, and my body relaxes slightly. He might be batshit crazy and dangerous, but in *this* moment, I breathe a little easier. Besides, there's no escaping here... At least for now.

"Why were you coming here?" he asks, surprising me by continuing the conversation. "Not *here*, but Colorado."

"Oh," I pause, the reminder sending a squeeze of heartache through my chest. "I was coming to spend the holiday with my boyfriend at his family's cabin. We, um, broke up over the phone when I was almost here—er, something like that." I don't know why I add it, but there's no taking it back once it's out.

His brows furrow as he flips the meat in the pan. "What was the address? There aren't any other cabins on this road for miles."

I purse my lips. "I'd have to look at my phone...I don't remember it."

"Mm," he mutters, turning his attention back to the stove. Disappointment rattles my chest at his reaction—like it bothers him I don't know. But why would he care? Why do *I* care?

"The visibility started to suck when I turned onto this road," I clarify, grabbing his attention again. "And my GPS told me I had twelve miles to go when I turned off the highway. It froze, and I couldn't get it to reload. I somehow ended up in the wrong driveway."

"There's no houses on this road," he says, setting the tongs down on the counter, angling his body to me. "The GPS had to have been leading you to the wrong place. It's not reliable out here. Your boyfriend should've known that." It's the most he's said since I arrived, and I find myself lost in the deep, commanding tone, my body reacting in a way that I *don't* like.

I swallow it and tighten my quads beneath the table. "I don't know. I just copied and pasted the address from his text."

He nods, shrugging to himself. "Strange."

Yeah, so is this. I take another deep breath and scan the walls, noticing how bare they are. There's not a picture in sight, but he's also an assumably single man living alone. No bachelor pad is ever impressive, but it does prompt me to take a risk.

"What's your name?" I ask, my heart leaping to my throat. "We never really, um, introduced ourselves and since—"

"Turner," he cuts me off before I start to ramble. He doesn't offer up a last name, and I don't press. Or maybe Turner *is* his last name? I don't know.

"I'm Em."

"Emersyn," he corrects me, and continues at my shocked expression. "I saw it on your driver's license."

"Right," I breathe out a sigh, trying to settle my fraying nerves again. "Most people call me Em."

"Okay."

Fuck me, this is awkward. I'm just as miserable as I am scared, and I let my mind run in the moment. *What would I be doing had I made it to Adam?* I frown at the thought. *We'd probably be fighting, and I'd be begging for the snow to clear so I could leave.*

How fucking ironic.

But at least I'd be safe. I steal a glance back at Turner, who's expression is downcast suddenly. Is he...*upset?* I can't tell, but he has a distant look on his face as he seems to go through the motions of finishing the food. *Should I keep talking?* I brush my hair out of my face. Why do I always need to keep talking?

"I haven't ever been stuck in a blizzard like this," I say, clearing my throat as he reaches into the cabinet, grabbing a couple of plates.

"You'll be stuck in another one in a couple days." He sets a steak on either plate, and then splits the mixed vegetables between them. "We're supposed to get multiple rounds of snow."

"Guess I might be here for Christmas," I chuckle.

He shrugs, and then picks up the plates and brings them to the table. He doesn't sit down though. He returns to the kitchen and grabs two waters, forks, and knives. His movements are almost *nervous*? It's hard to read him as he sets everything down and then pulls out the chair across from me.

"Do you have family around here?"

He stares at his plate, freezing at the question. "No." He shakes his head in a quick succession, and then begins to eat.

My hands still tremble as I retrieve the utensils and cut into the steak. "I don't like the holidays all that much anymore." I don't know why my mouth is still moving, but I'm desperate to make friends—or something.

"Yeah, happens." He forks a bite of broccoli into his mouth.

I nod, following suit. "Thank you for dinner," I say, swallowing.

He looks across the table at me, holding my gaze long enough for my heart to skip a few beats. "You're welcome, Em." His voice drops when he says my nickname, I hang on it, staring at his mouth.

I roll my lips together. "What do you like to do for fun?"

"I don't have fun," he chuckles, his knife slicing through the meat as he pauses. "But I used to do a lot of things."

"Yeah?" I don't press as to why he doesn't have fun anymore. I just focus on what he'll give me—like I read once in a book about a woman surviving a serial killer. Not that Turner is one. But he *could* be. "What did you do?"

"I liked to work out a lot," he says, shrugging.

"You look like you still do," I blurt.

He looks up at me, and I *swear* there's a brief flicker of amusement, but it fades to something distant. "I also liked music and concerts, trucks, work... Normal shit."

I smile softly. "You don't do any of that anymore?"

Turner shakes his head, his Adam's apple bobbing. "No. I stay here mostly."

"And you never leave?"

He hesitates, like he's about to say something first but holds off another few moments. "Not really. I used to though. This was my parents' cabin, then my brother's, then mine."

"I have a sister," I say, offering up something about myself to help with peeling back the layers of him. Something about him pulls at me, and that distance in his eyes is as alluring as it is unsettling. For some reason, I *want* to know more about him. Maybe it's the stereotypical draw of the mysterious stranger—or maybe it's that self-preservation kicking in. Keeping your enemy close or whatever.

But he's not an enemy, really. Or is he?

"You can sleep in my room," his voice interrupts my thoughts. "I shouldn't make you stay on the couch. I'll sleep there."

"You don't have to do that," I reason. "You're way too big for the couch."

"I'll sleep on the floor."

"Seems unfair," I say, cutting off a piece of steak and popping it in my mouth. It's definitely venison, based on the gamey flavor. Turner studies me as I chew and swallow. "It's good," I tell him, taking a gander that's what he was waiting for.

"It's edible."

I laugh. "Isn't that all that matters?"

"Yeah, I guess so."

And then he *almost* smiles again.

CHAPTER 7

TURNER

MAYBE THIS WON'T BE SO hard. She appears easy to please, and I like her laugh when it comes naturally. I finish what she doesn't, and she stands at the same time as me, picking up her own plate.

"I can do the dishes," she offers, holding out her hand to me. "It's only fair since you cooked."

"It'll go faster if we work together." I don't know why I say it. She seems surprised by any nicety I extend to her, and that makes sense. I'm a scary fucking asshole who shot her and knocked her around.

And I feel guilty as fuck for it right now.

"I need to change that," I gesture to the bandage on her hand. "It got wet in the shower, and I glued it shut. It needs air to heal."

"Oh, yeah," Emersyn shakes her head as she slips past me, her arm brushing mine. "I forgot about it. Let's just change it after dishes."

My core heats up at the momentary touch, and my mind conjures up an image of her bare beneath me. My hands tremble as I think about reaching out and brushing her skin again, the warmth of her against me. I forgot how good it could feel, and the more she talks—even if it's awkward and tense—the more I wonder what her full lips would taste like.

"I can wash if you want to dry?" she offers, her voice unsticking me from my mind. "Or vice versa?"

Everything is a question with her.

"It doesn't matter," I tell her as she grabs the pans from the stove and sets them in the sink. I don't know why I fight the urge to stare at her so much. It's probably because I haven't been around someone in so long, right? She's giving me a glimpse of what it might've been like to have someone... *if I was just different.* If I didn't end up killing any living person in my vicinity.

I shake it off and grab a towel, drying and putting everything away as she washes them. It doesn't take long before we're done, and I'm left in the kitchen there with her, handing her the towel so she can dry her hands. Afterwards, she hangs it on the handle of the oven, and then turns to retreat to the living room, where Gunner is camped out on the couch.

"Wait," I call after her. "I need to take care of your hand."

"I can just take the band aid off," she laughs, her voice light. She's trying so hard not to be a burden, and I almost feel guilty for what I told her earlier. But it's the truth. I didn't *want* her to be here. I still don't *really* want her here, but here she is.

And I want to touch her again.

"I'll do it."

Emersyn stills, and I notice the darkened spot on her sweater from the water at the sink. "Okay, fine." She approaches me, stopping a foot away and extending her injured hand.

Heart pounding in my ears, I take her wrist in my hand and peel back the bandage with the other. She doesn't wince, and I take in the burned flesh around the closed gash, the sight beckoning me backward. I don't hear what she says then. All I hear is the click of a magazine and screams lighting up in my ears, exhilaration taking over body. My mouth grows dry, and my gut furls with impending excitement.

I should tell her to run. Run as far and as fast as she can.

I drop her hand as Gunner's collar jingles, and within seconds, he's there, pawing at my leg. I blow out a sharp breath, and the desire to play war fades from my mind. Gunner's whine replaces my mind's chaos as I stroke the black fur on his head.

"Are you okay?" her voice comes next, and I don't know what the fuck I'm supposed to tell her. No one ever asks me that. Not anymore.

"Yeah, he just needs to go out," I clear my throat, avoiding her gaze as I lead him toward the back door. The back porch is screened in, and while it's cold as fuck, duty calls. Gunner has to do his business on artificial turf, but it's better than nothing. I swing the door open, the sharp winds whipping through the house.

I don't look back at her as I step outside with my dog. I don't think she has any idea of the threat looming here. It's better that she doesn't. I take a long breath. The way the sharp breeze cuts through my shirt reminds me that I'm still fucking alive, and I close my eyes. Having her here is a good exercise of self-control, and I could use the restraint training. Maybe she *is* a challenge.

"Do you want a coat?" Emersyn sticks her head out the door, her nose scrunched up. "It's freezing out here."

I shake my head. "No."

Her green eyes tug at me, and grief of my reality threatens to take hold. She's got this new way of making me not like being a trigger-happy lunatic. "Are you sure?"

"Yeah, you should go to bed." My tone is rough, and borderline condescending. I know I sound like an asshole, but she doesn't realize I thought of killing her a few minutes ago.

"I'm not really tired."

I glare at her, shaking my head. "I didn't ask if you were tired."

She doesn't say anything to that, and as the winds howl and snow blows, she disappears back inside. The door closes quietly, and I stay outside with Gunner for a few moments longer, letting him finish. He'd been a gift from my brother when I was discharged...

And I wonder, if even from six feet under, he still thinks the damn dog would fix me.

"If he only knew," I grunt, my eyes casting out toward the place where all my sins are buried beneath the snow. I zone out for a few beats, and then when my fingers grow numb, I head back inside, taking in the room.

Her bags are gone, and my guess is that she lugged them to my room. The only signs of her are the pair of jeans and women's hiking shoes by the fire. She missed those. My eyes dart down the hallway as I pass it, making my way to the kitchen. I turn the light off, and let the house fall into darkness aside from the fire—but even that is dying down.

Checking the time, it's late enough I could sleep. However...That's also when the worst of my urges have always started. It all starts with me going to bed, and then I wake up, lost in my head.

With another warm body in the house, will it trigger me?

I eye the bedroom door and then glance back at Gunner. If I have any shot of not killing her, I need the bottle of pills from the nightstand. I haven't slept since Emersyn arrived, and things will only get worse if I keep putting it off.

I'll just have to go get them.

Because you know, of course, being sleep deprived can be a trigger, too. Fuck, in the right setting, *anything* can set me off, especially when I'm on edge. I take in a deep breath and push forward, heading down the hallway to the bedroom door. I knock twice on the door, and then wait.

Within seconds, it swings open, Emersyn in the threshold. She peers up at me, curiosity in her gaze. The low light dances across her face, mixing with shadows, but I can see make out the light splash of freckles on her face. She's growing on me. And I know that's a bad thing. She clears her throat—and I realize I've been staring at her like a fucking creep.

"I just need to get something," I say, eyeing her as she steps to the side. "Then I'll be upstairs for the rest of the night." I don't know why I tell her that, and honestly, I'm starting to get loose lipped with her.

"You really don't have to sleep on the floor," she reasons. "I can sleep on the couch or something."

"I don't sleep a lot, so it's fine." I make my way to the nightstand, ripping it open and pulling out the bottle of sleeping pills. "And with these, I can sleep anywhere." I mean it as a joke, but it comes out so fucking flat that she just stares at me blankly.

Jeez, I'm bad at this. Gripping the bottle, I shut the drawer, and head back for the door.

"What's your dog's name?" she calls after me, and the tone of her voice causes me to pause instead of ignoring her. There's something desperate underlaying her generic question. I recognize it, and spin around to face her. Her arms are wrapped around herself, and even though I find her presence a nuisance and her questions annoying, there's something admirable about the way she just doesn't stop talking.

I wonder if she'd understand I also have unstoppable habits.

"Gunner. He's ten. Getting up there in age." I sound so awkward and so pathetic I could bang my head against the wall. I used to know how to talk to people. I used to fucking *flirt.* Now, I can barely talk and not sound like an imbecile.

"Is he a service dog?"

"Excuse me?" I shoot back at her, offended. "Why the fuck would I need a *service* dog?" She's making assumptions.

And it pisses me off.

"I noticed him pawing at you..." Her voice trails off. "I thought maybe... Your expression changed... I—"

"You, what?" I growl as my hand is suddenly wrapped around her throat, her pulse throbbing against my finger. "You think I'm fucking crazy? Huh? Why don't you run your mouth a little more?"

"I'm s-s-sorry," she chokes out, her teeth suddenly chattering.

I catch a hint of her sweet scent and guide her backward until her ass hits the side of the bed. Forcing her to sit down, which damn near puts her face cock level, I growl, "How sorry *are* you, Emersyn?"

She swallows, biting down on her lip. "Very?"

I tilt my head, studying the confusing expression on her face. She's scared, that's for sure, but there's something else in the mix...*intrigue,* maybe? Hard to say.

"Who I am, is none of your business," I bite, tipping her chin back. "Got it?"

"Okay," she whispers, her eyes boring into mine. Something in my chest rattles at the look there—the unrelenting softness and the way she's searching my face. It's like she's *trying* to understand me.

And now, I'm the one confused.

"It's okay, Turner." Her tone is achingly sweet. "I won't ask you anymore questions."

I can't conjure up a response. Everything is wrong in my

head right now. And before I can stop myself, I'm leaning down, brushing my lips across her jaw. My cock grows rock hard as she shivers against my touch. I wait for her to pull away from my lips on my skin, but she only lets out a sharp breath.

What a good, weak girl.

My thoughts grow dark and lustful. She's so fucking easy, moldable, even. Could I keep her as my own?

"What do you want from me?" Emersyn whispers, her voice barely audible as I pause, my grip loosening.

I rest my head against hers. "I don't know."

Emersyn's breaths are ragged, and it sparks a new kind of excitement in me. My mind races. *Is she wet for me? Does she want me? How far can I go before I snap?* I thread my fingers through her hair and tip her head back, sliding my other hand from her throat and down her body. I suddenly want to dance with the fucking Devil.

"Here's your chance, Emersyn," I taunt her as I graze her breasts. "Tell me no, and I'll think about it, but..." I catch her gaze. "Part of me thinks you're as turned on as I am right now."

Her lips part as I dip lower, reaching the button of her jeans. "St-stop."

Fuck.

"Why?" I demand, my exhilaration growing ragey in its cage. "Why should I stop? Do you not want this? Because I have a feeling you want it."

"My boyfriend—"

"Isn't your boyfriend right now," I cut her off, unsnapping the button. "We're trapped in this house, *Em...*" *You're either going to end up fucked or dead. Or both. Not sure yet if fucking will be enough to stave off my madness.*

"I don't know... I don't really know you..."

I let out a frustrated sigh. *Fucking fine.* I'll just go to sleep. I drop her back and stalk from the room, grabbing the pills I left sitting on the dresser. I thunder up the stairs, the echo of my footsteps barely audible over the anger humming in my mind.

I slam the lookout door behind me, Gunner barely slipping inside, and then I flip the lock. I open the pill bottle, and shake out a handful, popping them into my mouth and dry swallowing. I set the nearly empty bottle on the desk and retreat to the corner, taking a seat on the carpet and leaning my head back against the wall.

Fuck her for saying no. Fuck me for not killing her. Fuck me for not knowing how to be a normal human being anymore.

Closing my eyes, I let the chill sink in, the draft providing me with the cold shoulder I desire right now. Gunner sits beside me as the heaviness takes hold, drawing me into an unconscious stupor that numbs my brain and body.

It's the only time I ever get any peace.

I just hope it lasts a while.

CHAPTER 8

EMERSYN

I STARE AT THE STAIRWELL, counting six treads before the mid-landing is swallowed by darkness. Turner and his dog disappeared up those stairs almost two freaking days ago, and I haven't seen either of them since. Luckily, when I had followed him out onto the back porch, I'd found the stack of firewood, which has allowed me to keep the cabin warm. But...*where is he?*

My jaw tenses as I think about the pill bottle he grabbed, and the way he pushed me sexually right before. I *hate* how turned on I was by him, and part of me regrets not letting him wipe the breakup from my mind momentarily. Part of me is still hoping Adam will want to work things out—but the smarter part knows it needs to be over.

Maybe Turner could jump start that process.

If he's even still alive.

I frown at the intrusive thought, but honestly, it's been flickering beneath the surface ever since he took that pill bottle and never came back. And I mean, maybe he's just keeping to himself? Maybe he's totally fine up there—wherever *there* is.

But I can't let it go.

His dog should at least need to go to the bathroom? Eat? Something. I smooth out my sweater and take a step toward the stairs. *If he's up there, and wants to be left alone, I'll just apologize and come back. No big deal.* But as the wood creaks beneath my steps, it *feels* like a big deal. It feels like I might be walking right into a trap.

Taking deep breaths to steady my racing heart, I pause on the mid-landing. I check my now-charged watch, noting that it's almost dark outside, too, which probably isn't helping this whole escapade I've started on. But I continue forward, my mind running one hundred miles an hour.

What will I do if he...isn't okay? I don't have a phone. He doesn't have a phone. How do I get help?

As I reach the top of the stairs, I'm met with multiple doors—all of them closed. I stand there for a few long moments, straining to hear something other than the howling of the winds. The snow fall has slowed from what I can tell, but the wind keeps whipping violently. As if on cue, a draft causes a chill to run down my spine, and I wrap my arms around myself.

I make it to the first door and stop again. *Do I knock? Or just open it?* I want to shout out my frustration. I'm already freaking trapped in a stranger's house in the middle of a fucking blizzard—with no phone—and now I'm having to do a welfare check on the guy who knocked me out. I don't know if I'm supposed to be terrified or just...*mad*. Regardless, I choose to knock softly.

But nothing happens.

I try the doorknob, and it turns in my hand. I push the door in, but the room is completely dark. I can't make out what's on the shelves and walls, but it's easy to see that Turner and his dog are MIA. I close the door and move to the next one. As I do, the sound of a slight whining catches my attention from the next door over. I creep across to it, my heart pounding in my ears now.

And then I knock twice, just like before.

Holding my breath, I wait, listening to the whining intensify on the other side of the door. It causes me to nearly panic when Turner doesn't come to answer. I knock again, this time, twice as loud.

"Turner," I call out, my voice rasping from the silence I've been living in. "Are you okay?"

More fucking whining.

"Turner," I say it louder, and then go for the doorknob. It *doesn't* turn in my hand. It's locked. I jiggle the doorknob; now almost positive I'm just going to find a dead body on the other side. Hands shaking, I lean down to scrutinize the lock, but it's a pinhole. I don't have the right tool to unlock it.

I choke back a cry, before turning to head back downstairs. I might be able to find something to jimmy it open with. I mean, at this point, it's probably a medical emergency, right? I glance down to my wool socks and fill my lungs with oxygen, trying to keep myself from having a panic attack.

I'm fine. I can handle this. I'll find something to open the door and then—

The door clicks from behind me. I spin around to see the door swing open and Gunner rush out. He bounds to me, his butt wiggling with excitement, but I can barely focus on him as Turner appears in the hallway, running his hands over his face.

His eyes widen as he sees me, like somehow, he didn't expect me to be here. "What're you doing up here?"

Are you fucking kidding me right now?

My jaw drops as my hands fall to my sides. "Uh, looking for you? It's been almost two fucking days since I saw you last, and I thought that..." I can't bring myself to finish the thought, realizing how over-the-top I'd sound. I look away and let out a sigh. "I just wanted to make sure you were okay."

"I see," he grunts, eyeing me as he takes a step closer. He's in the same clothes that he was in the night he disappeared, and the closer he comes, the more disheveled he appears. His face is pale and his eyes bloodshot. His shoulders slumped. "I just needed to catch up on sleep."

"For two fucking days?" I blurt out, unable to hide my concern. "I don't know how you...I don't..." I can't find the words as he nears me, his chocolate eyes holding mine.

"I should be good for a while now. No worries." He slips past me, his arm brushing mine, and heads for the stairs behind me, Gunner following in step with him.

I stand there in a stupor. What the fuck did he do up here for two days? He doesn't *look* like he got all that much sleep. I glance over my shoulder as his figure disappears down the stairwell and then turn back, shaking my head. He went from coming onto me, to just... *this?*

Who the hell am I snowed in with?

After a few minutes, I spin on my heels and head back down the stairs, thankful for the warmth that comes with hitting ground level. My leggings are fleece lined, but the cabin I was planning to stay in with Adam had central heat— and if this cabin has it, I wouldn't know.

I glance around for Turner, halfway wishing he was back upstairs. Not that it would help me sleep at night. My sleep is restless and fitful, leaving my head aching when I wake up in the morning. The back door slams as Gunner comes bounding through, followed by Turner.

"The snow is slowing down," he tells me, rubbing his eyes. "But the second storm will move in tomorrow."

"Ah, yeah." My shoulders slump. "Another storm. Right."

He nods, rubbing the back of his neck and grimacing. "Yeah. That's what I said." Gunner jumps up on the couch, circling until he gets comfortable, but I can barely take my eyes off Turner, standing just a few feet away. There's stubble aligning his sharp jaw, and despite his brawny figure, he appears ragged.

What happened to you?

I want to ask him. I want to know if he's always been like this. He mentioned he had hobbies and a life, so maybe at one point, he wasn't. I try to imagine him without the edge —the rugged unstableness. I get lost in the image, and it's only as he clears his throat that I realize I'm blocking his path.

"I need to shower."

"Right, sorry." I angle my body to side, as he steps past me. "Are you hungry?"

He stops, gazing back at me. "Yeah, but I can make dinner. I owe you."

I furrow my brow as he disappears into the bedroom and shuts the door. I have no idea what the hell is going on. I shake my head, pushing my hair out of my face. It's exhausting being here, and the sooner I can leave, the better off I'll be... But there's no way I'll ever forget this strange man. I take a seat next to Gunner on the couch, stroking his dark fur.

"He's not okay, is he?" I ask, sighing. Gunner lets out a heavy breath, as if to answer the question. I listen to the sound of the shower running, and imagine Turner beneath the stream of water, washing away two days' worth of mystery. I clench my thighs at my body's reaction, and then roll my eyes at myself.

He's a bad, bad *idea.*

Twenty minutes later, Turner reappears, this time dressed in a pair of dark wash jeans and a gray henley. His dark hair is damp as he steps into the kitchen, the soft glow glistening against the moisture. He's quiet as he goes through the motions of shoving some sort of casserole into the oven, and I'm left to watch him from afar.

I fight the urge to talk and fill the silence, but instead I choose to wait it out, my uncertainty stronger than my need to speak. Turner appears to set a timer on the oven, and then surprisingly, he joins me in the living room.

"I see you managed," his deep voice gravels as he takes a seat in the arm chair across from me. "I didn't realize how long I was up there."

"Yeah, I was fine." I watch him cautiously, my heart skipping over itself as his eyes linger on my face. "I just got a little worried."

He seems taken by this, his brows creasing. "Why?"

I purse my lips. "Because you were MIA for almost two days. That's a long time to go without eating or something..."

Surprisingly, he chuckles. "You're lying."

I swallow the knot in my throat, running my hands down my thighs. "I don't know what you mean."

"Why were you worried?"

"You were missing for two days," I repeat myself, my voice tinged with frustration. "That's a valid reason to be worried."

"Because I hadn't eaten?"

"Because you could've been dead," I blurt out, ignoring the smirk on his handsome fucking face.

Turner leans forward, resting his elbows on his knees. "It would take a lot more to kill me, Emersyn. Trust me."

"Good to know," I mutter, my chest heaving as I catch a whiff of his new cologne and force my eyes away. "I'll make a note of that."

He cocks a brow at me. "Interesting thing to take note of."

"You're really picking apart every word that comes out of my mouth," I shoot back at him. "Like I'm the one who disappeared for two days."

Turner shrugs but his gaze darkens as he catches mine again. "I kind of like you all worked up, *Em*."

My lips part but nothing comes out as Turner stands to his feet, leaving me there on the couch to watch him walk away. My eyes follow him all the way back to the kitchen. I don't want to admit what his words did to me—or how he affected me in the bedroom that night—but when I shift to get more comfortable, the dampness in between my legs tells the story.

And it's the fastest I've *ever* been turned on.

There is something wrong with me. He's probably going to kill me, and here I am, getting turned on and growing attached.

I bite down on my lip as he leans against the counter, folding his arms across his broad chest. He's closed off and complicated, but it doesn't stop me from wanting to know more about him so badly. I don't even have a good reason as to why, either. There's something dangerous about him, but also something broken...

And I'm drawn to it more than I want to admit.

My mind fills with the image of him touching me, and it startles me as much as it turns me on more. Turner is a walking red flag, but the moment his eyes soften in my direction, all the sirens grow silent—and that is almost as terrifying as this blizzard. I inwardly chide myself.

It's just because I want a rebound... That's it. It has to be.

CHAPTER 9

TURNER

I MADE HER BLUSH, and after two days of in and out of consciousness, I'm feeling a little better. She came looking for me, and it's strangely a compliment of sorts. Sure, had I overdosed, she would've found my forty-eight-hour decaying corpse, but no one has searched for me in years.

She came looking after two days, and it wasn't because she was struggling to get the fire going or needing help. She was just worried...*about me.*

And that's all I can think about as I sit across from her at the table, sharing the shitty chicken parm frozen casserole dinner. I didn't feel like putting in effort when it came to eating, but I wasn't going to make her cook, either.

"It's shit, I know," I say as she forks a bite of the spaghetti.

She shrugs. "I've had worse."

"Tell me what's worse. Tell me the worst thing you've ever eaten."

Emersyn cracks a smile. "Um, probably the time I ate at a seafood restaurant and the fish was undercooked."

"You can eat fish raw," I reason. "So, it might've tasted like shit, but at least it wasn't going to kill you."

She narrows her pretty jade eyes at my smirk. "Unless it hadn't been stored right."

"Well, glad you survived it." I chuckle, my body feeling a lot lighter ever since getting some sleep. I know I can't let my guard down, but I feel okay. No strong desire to murder her in a war-raged blackout. My head is clear, and hell, I'm sharing my table with an attractive woman—one that I can't stop fucking staring at. Maybe it's the fact that we're snowed in or that I haven't been around someone in so long, but it *feels* like more than that. She charges the air around me.

"What's the worst thing you've ever eaten?" She sets her fork down beside the nearly finished meal.

"Uh, I don't know." I shift in my chair. "My mom's meatloaf probably."

"Oh, that's just mean," she laughs, shocking my chest with her light and airy tone. "Your poor mother."

"At six feet under, I don't think she's worried about it now." I frown, killing my own goddamn good mood. Emersyn falls into silence for a few moments, and I start to hate myself all over again.

"I'm sorry for your loss," she finally says.

I ignore it, hating that phrase but choosing not to let her know that. She's got no idea of my life. I scrape my fork across the plate. "What about your family?" Maybe if she just talks about herself, we can avoid the subject of me.

"What about them?" She leans her chin against her hand, her brows creased ever so slightly. The gesture is small, but it catches my attention. My cock strains as my mind flashes with her beneath me, making that exact same face as I press into her pussy.

Sleep didn't fix that issue, apparently.

"Turner?"

"Sorry," I grunt. "Uh, I just meant for you to tell me about your family. I don't know." I force my eyes down to my food, the sight of it instantly draining my arousal.

"Oh, well, my parents are still together after like forty years of marriage. I think they're annoyed that I still haven't met the right person yet. Well, I mean, I thought I had. They thought I had, too..." Her voice trails off, and I tip my gaze back to her, hating what I see.

"This must be the ex-boyfriend?" A pang of envy rattles my chest, and I'm reminded of all the ways that I fall short yet again. My body might be strong, but my mind is a fucking bomb waiting to explode—and take her with me.

"Yeah, Adam," she gives me his name like I give a shit. "I thought we were going to his family's cabin for him to fix things."

"Hmm."

"Yeah, it was a pipe dream," she scoffs, shaking her head. "I was stupid for thinking it could be fixed. We've been rocky for almost a year, and I was grasping at straws. It's been so tumultuous, and then my best friend called me on my way here—just to tell me that he told his brother we're not going anywhere and it was all for looks."

I nod, trying to empathize with something that sounds so...*pitiful.* "But you broke up with him, yeah?"

She holds my gaze from across the table. "Yeah. I broke up with him, and then ended up here. He told me he was coming to get me—and that he didn't mean what he told his brother."

"Ah, so you'll be good with him then," I say the words like they're poisonous.

"No, I don't think so. I'm getting too old to deal with the bullshit. I just want someone to really commit. I'm tired of the games."

"Wouldn't know anything about that." I drum my fingers on the table and then push back, grabbing our plates.

She follows my lead. "So you don't date, I take it?"

I smile with my back turned to her. "Hard to date anyone when you live alone in the woods." *And have an addiction to murder.*

"There's a town like an hour or so from here though, right?"

"I never go," I chuckle, scraping off the remnants of dinner into Gunner's bowl. I don't usually feed him left-overs, but I'm sure as shit not going to be eating anymore of this.

"Why don't you go?"

I hesitate, choosing my answer wisely. "I don't like crowds. Or people."

"But you're letting me stay here."

I set the dishes down in the sink, angling my body toward her. "I really *didn't* let you stay here. I just chose not to let you freeze to death. Let's not forget how tense our first meeting was."

Her eyes flash with what I recognize as fear. "Right."

"Yeah, so don't get too comfortable," I snort, turning on the water and beginning to wash the dishes. Guilt throttles me, but I ignore it. *Why am I so fucked up?*

"Noted." Emersyn takes it as a joke, laughing. She grabs a towel and dries the dishes as I wash them, putting them up in their places. Once we're finished, Emersyn escapes to the bedroom, returning with a silver laptop tucked under her arm.

"I don't have internet," I say flatly.

She waves me off. "I know, my computer didn't pick up any Wi-Fi. But I was thinking we could listen to music? You said you haven't listened in years, right?"

"Uh..." I hesitate, my stomach feeling knotted. "I guess."

"Cool." She sets the computer on the table, and I stand a few feet away, borderline nervous as to what the hell she's going to play.

"What genre do you like?" Emersyn looks up over the top of the computer. "My guess is you're not in the holiday mood?"

"Uh... I don't know." I can't even *think* of anything. "Why don't you just play me *your* favorite song?"

"Hmm." She rolls her lips and nods, her attention falling back to the computer. I watch her as she scrolls, and I start to admire the little things—the way her hair is tucked behind her right ear, the way her lips are pursed as she focuses, and

the way she lights up when she finally finds something. It's...
cute.

The sound of a piano fills my ears, and I tense as the tune
carries, picking up with a deep male voice. It's not nearly as
miserable as I figured it'd be, and my breaths slow as it fills
the cabin.

"Do you like it?" she asks me, her brows raising with an
innocent eagerness.

I nod. "Yeah, it's not bad."

"I bet you listen to rap or something," Em tips her head
back and laughs. It's surreal having her in my kitchen,
tapping her purple sock to the beat of the music. She's so
fucking oblivious to the danger she's in, and maybe I can
pretend like I am, too—just enough to enjoy life for an
evening. "So is it rap?"

"Not really. I liked metal, but I haven't..." *Damnit, she's
going to think I'm fucking nuts.* "I haven't heard anything in
years."

She pauses. "You mean, you haven't listened to music in
years? Or just metal?"

"Music," I answer her, my voice barely audible over the
hum of some guy singing about how shitty humankind is.

"How many years?"

I swallow my pride, forcing the honesty. "A decade probably." I don't like to miss my old self too much.

She gapes. "Wow. Is that how long you've been here?"

"Pretty much."

"How old are you?" She blurts it out, and I try not to

close off. She's not likely to make it out of here, so who cares if she knows the truth?

"I turn forty-one in January."

The music fades to silence as she speaks. "So, you've been here since you were thirty-one?"

"Yeah, thirty-one or thirty-two, I think," I say, unable to clarify the timeline in my own head. "Something like that. I don't keep up with the details."

Her face twists, morphing into a painful sympathy. "Wow, so you... You've been disconnected for that long?"

"I mean, I wouldn't say I'm stuck in 2013," I try to laugh at my dishonorable discharge date, but honestly, it fucking hurts to think about the way I used to think I was normal back then.

"I was in college," she says the words painfully soft.

"Yeah?" I shift to my heels, desperate to change the subject. "What'd you study?"

"I switched my major so many times, I couldn't tell you. I dropped out when I got a decent job. I was too busy chasing a social life."

I chuckle, trying to relax. "Like men, you mean?"

"Kind of, I guess. I got married super young, then divorced. All that happened during that time. I was a handful, immature, I think." Emersyn frowns, and then shakes her head. "I was the toxic one, that's for sure. I was working through my own insecurities back then. I had horrible taste, and I was too clingy."

"I was toxic at that age, too," I admit. "I didn't slow

down until I was in my mid-twenties, but then I started having to do other things to, um..."

"Cope?"

My throat tightens. "Yeah, I guess." I prepare for more questions—ones that I'm not sure I can answer. However, she doesn't press. Instead, Emersyn double clicks and starts a new song. I don't recognize it.

She looks up at me, something in her eyes as she speaks carefully. "Did you ever dance?"

"Uh..." I feel frozen, my heart picking up at the thought of being close to her. Normally, I would *never* even consider it, but she's... She's *getting* to me, and I *like* the way I feel right now. Again, maybe I could just let myself enjoy tonight. "Do you *want* to dance or something?" I feel like a middle schooler.

She laughs softly, but there's sadness in her eyes. "I don't dance. I never really had. No one dances with me."

"Start it over," I tell her, my body throbbing with a new kind of anxiety.

She raises her brow, and does as I say, and then steps around the counter. "Okay..."

"Okay," I say stupidly as I try to discreetly wipe my hands on my jeans. I take hers, and it's cold in my grip, but her skin is soft against mine.

She steps into me, her other hand on my shoulder, and somehow, I find her waist. My heart fucking throbs in my temple as I hold her close, swaying to music. Muscle memory kicks in, and I let it lead, zoning out in the sweet scent of shea butter coming from her hair. I inhale it like it's oxygen, knowing this could easily be the last time I have a chance to hold someone like this. She'd never let me this close if she knew.

But I don't want to let her go.

"What song is this?" I choke out, feeling irrevocably human.

"*The Only Thing Left,*" she answers me softly. "By Vincent Lima."

I nod and then hold her tighter, leaning in and resting my cheek against her temple. Closing my eyes, I cling to the moment with her, knowing that when I'm burying her body in the snow, I'll replay this moment over and over again.

And maybe it'll be enough to finally put this all to an end. It's always been the plan once Gunner is gone. He's the only reason I'm still here. Once he's gone, there's no reason for me to remain in this realm.

As the song ends, my thoughts still and I expect her pull away—but she doesn't. The next song starts. It's not a slow song, and I recognize the pop singer's voice but not the song itself. Emersyn starts to giggle like a kid and starts dancing...

Like goofy fucking dancing.

I burst into laughter as she sings it to me, dancing and holding onto my hand. She has a decent voice but no rhythm. Her light brown hair bounces against her shoulders, and the smile on her face exudes so much light and happiness. She's fucking beautiful, and she's in *my* house, her eyes glistening with amusement mirroring my own.

As it hits the bridge, a deeper, sultrier hum, the air charges, her eyes daring me. My fingers are still intertwined with hers. My heart beats unevenly with nerves, and I pull her into my chest, my fingers threading through her soft hair. My nose brushes hers, but my lips are faster than I expect, driven by a strong desire.

And holy fuck.

She kisses me back, parting to let me devour her mouth entirely. My cock grows rigid against her stomach, and anything I am and or ever was fades to black. All I can think about is *her.* I sweep my hand down her side, and she stumbles back at my force, letting out a moan as I lift her into the air.

Her ass lands on the butcherblock countertop, and she cries out as the new arrangement allows my cock to press right against her clothed center. An unrecognizable groan erupts from my throat as I grind into her, my tongue still interlaced with hers. My fingertips brush over the bare skin of her neck, floating down as they rest on her collarbone.

I want to shred her fucking clothes as I grip the back of her head, holding her against me, nipping at her bottom lip. It's a primal desire, bubbling up and taking control of my entire body. As she rolls her hips against me, I growl in desperation and drop my hand to my jeans.

But then Gunner barks.

And I freeze. He *never* barks.

Not unless someone is out there.

CHAPTER 10

EMERSYN

TURNER'S entire body stiffens against mine as Gunner's bark resounds through the cabin for a second time. "It's stopped snowing," he mutters into me, his voice husky from the charged moment between us. Disappointment pangs in my chest and my shoulders slump as he untangles from me.

I graze my lips with my fingers, the flesh swollen, as Turner heads for Gunner, perched at the front door. He peers through one of the windows, and the dog barks again. I stand there, watching, hot and bothered. I didn't mean for anything to happen between us, but...*his kiss*. I lost control the moment his mouth collided with mine—and I'm trying not to focus on the way that's never happened before.

I've never slept around. I'm the kind of girl who gets emotionally attached, and then falls in love too fast. After that, I either get heartbroken or fall out as fast as I fell in. But still, I've never been kissed like that... Like I was oxygen, and he was suffocating.

"Stay here," Turner's voice breaks my thoughts, and I realize he's fully dressed in his white camo to go out. "Don't come out. No matter what."

I furrow my brow, my anxiety growing as I note the gun in his hands. "Why? Are you going to—"

His eyes hold mine. "Just don't come outside, Em."

"Okay," I choke out as he rips the front door open, and he and the dog disappear into the night. It slams behind him, and I jump at the sound. *What could possibly be out there? Adam? A search team? Is he going to murder them?* He's clearly the type to shoot first and ask questions later.

I run to the window, and peer out into the darkness. I can't see anything at all. I squint, unable to even find Turner or Gunner. I think about upstairs and remember the windows I saw from outside. It's a better vantage point. Out of caution, I slide on my hiking boots and grab my parka, and then head for the stairs.

My footsteps echo as race to the second floor. I stop at the first door, and push it open, met with darkness. I squint as I make my way to the window, ripping open the curtains and gazing out. There's nothing to see other than the shadow of trees. There's no moon or stars in the sky, no beams of flashlights or headlights. I give it up, choosing to back away from the window with a defeated sigh.

I'll just have to wait.

I turn around, my eyes having adjusted. They land on bookshelves, picture frames adorning the exterior portion. My curiosity gets the best of me, and I slip toward the door, finding the light switch. I flip it on, illuminating the entirety of the room, layered in dust.

My lips purse as I'm met with a completely different version of Turner. With my back against the door, I inch it shut until it clicks. Then, I start making my way around the room. Books line the shelves, but it's the pictures that catch my attention. He's young, smiling, and has his arms wrapped around his friends— or maybe brothers? It's hard to know in the first picture.

The next frame is a shadow box with Marine Raider patches. Next to it is a medal of honor and a photo of Turner receiving it. My brows furrow as I note the date. Thirteen years ago. I brush my fingers over the glass, glancing down at dark gray dust that coat them.

As I continue, I begin to shape his life in my mind. Most of the pictures on the shelves are of him and another few guys—one of them looking *so* much like Turner, himself. I keep making my way, seeing a lot of photos of him in his uniform in desert terrain.

When I reach the end of the first wall, I come to another shadow box—but it's not Turner's. It's someone named Taylor Martin, and it doesn't take me long to understand the purple heart.

Taylor Hart Martin, killed in the line of duty.

"Thirteen years ago," I say aloud, glancing back to the other. I don't have to know the details to put some of it together. I get it. He lost his brother, and as I keep going through the other *in memory of* décor, I realize he lost a lot more than just his blood brother.

My heart sinks deep in my chest as I make it down the second wall, seeing the pictures shift to family photos of Turner as a kid. I stop at the first one, seeing his presumed parents and three boys. I pick him out as the middle, and the one who passed as the youngest.

And then I find his father's obituary.

And mother's.

Date of Death: October 27, 2011.

I shake my head at the notion, and then go back to his brother's shadow box. *Killed in the line of duty, October 12, 2011.* My hand flies to my mouth. *Holy shit.* He lost his brother *and* his parents in the same freaking month? How could anyone be so fucking unlucky? My stomach churns with empathetic nausea. I take a deep breath and stop there, seeing a college degree hanging on the wall near the window.

Thomas Robert Martin.

I run my hands over my face. That must be the *other* brother? Is this his house? I mean, *his* degree is hanging on the wall. God knows what Turner went through. No wonder he locked himself away from the world. My eyes land on a typewritten letter, laying on the far corner desk then.

I shouldn't pry anymore.

I take a step toward it. However, I freeze when I hear a creak from outside the room. *Shit. Shit. Shit.*

The door flies open before I can move, and Turner's frame fills the doorway. He's still dressed in his winter gear, and there's *still* a rifle in his hands.

"What the *fuck* are you doing?" he explodes, his voice causing me to shrink backward.

I hold my hands up in surrender, but notice his eyes are elsewhere, taking in the pictures on the shelves. "Turner, I'm sorry...I was just trying to see out the window—"

"Get out." He raises the rifle, pointing it the center of my chest. His eyes are dark. And empty. Focused only on my chest. *"Get out."*

"Okay," I choke on the word, my heart in my ears. But I can't leave. He's blocking the door. "I just...I just need to slip by you."

He doesn't budge and as I gather the courage to meet his gaze, his eyes snap back to mine... But they're so... *dead.*

"Turner..." My voice trails off. "I'm sorry."

But it's like he doesn't hear me, even as he takes another step toward me. The barrel of his rifle is only a few feet from me now, and I feel tears welling up in my eyes. I stagger backward and to the right, trying to dodge the end of his gun.

And that's when it fires.

A scream lights up my lungs, and I lunge for the door as a second shot sounds. Panic sears through my body as I hear the bolt action from somewhere behind me.

"Get out!" Turner shouts.

His voice sounds like he's shouting above the volume level of a concert, but shots just keep going off, shaking the walls of the cabin. As I stumble down the stairs, I nearly crash into Gunner, who's running *toward* the sound of Turner shouting from behind me.

As I make it to the kitchen, the sound of upbeat pop music still playing in the chaos, I hear his thundering footsteps coming down the stairs. He continues to shout the same two words over and over. I don't get it. But I *do* understand the sound of another two rounds firing off from the stairwell.

He's going to fucking kill me.

Gripping my parka, I make a dash for the front door, ripping it open to the chilly air outside. The wind is so harsh that it burns as I take off into the deep snow. It buries me up to my knees, and I cry out in frustration as the shots keep sounding from behind me. Gunner starts barking, and all I can think about is making it to my truck.

Maybe I can dig it out and hide.

But is that an obvious place?

I spot a barn in the opposite direction, and part of me thinks of trying to go that way, but I realize no matter what, Turner has the upper hand. He's ex-special forces for fuck's sake. At best, I can run a mile in ten minutes and go hunting a few times a year, which just consists of sitting in a deer stand. I'm no fucking match for him.

It's a sobering thought—almost as sobering as dancing with him in the kitchen only an hour ago. I trudge forward, trying to remember where the hell the driveway is. The wind blows, and I can't tell if another round has gone off, or if it's just in my head. As soon as I make it to the tree line, I stop and pull on my coat.

I peer back toward the house, expecting to see Turner on the front porch like the first afternoon. But he's not there. My teeth chatter as I pull my hood up, my legs burning from my already soaked jeans. I squeeze my eyes shut, just long enough to gather my wits.

Everything is silent. Not a single natural noise fills the woods, and I don't know if that's a good or bad thing. I tighten the strap around my face to hold the hood, and start deeper into the woods, the sound of Gunner's bark jarring me.

Please don't lead him to me.

Tears slide down my cheeks as I trek into the darkness. Another shot fires, and this time, it sounds as if it's farther away. I breathe a little easier, but refrain from slowing my pace. *When did Turner say it would start to snow again? Tomorrow?*

My lips burn, the brutal winds reminding me of the kiss I was lost in—with a man who's now trying to kill me. I shiver beneath my coat, my eyes feeling tired as I try to navigate the unknown. I'm not used to this kind of snow. I let my mind loose to distract me.

Fuck you, Adam. It's your fault I'm here.

You should've just broken up with me when you decided it was going nowhere.

I bat the tears away. I have no right to be broken up about him. I mean, I was *just* kissing someone else—not even thinking about my newly ex-boyfriend. I could reason that I let Turner kiss me because it was a distraction from Adam, but the moment Turner started to open up, I haven't been able to recall those feelings for Adam.

It was over a long time ago.

I purse my lips, annoyed by my inability to retain feelings once someone starts pulling away. It's easier to break my own heart, and that's what I did with Adam. A year ago, he wouldn't answer the commitment questions.

And so, I started letting him go right then and there.

The moment things go wrong, I mentally bolt, even if I stay there physically. I frown at that—and the sound of a familiar voice. My heart stops as I take in the small clearing and the headlights shining through the night.

Adam.

CHAPTER 11

TURNER

WHAT THE HELL is going on?

With shaking hands, I hit the ground floor, my ears ringing as Gunner jumps at me, knocking some sense into my mind. Rage without known reason sears through my veins. I feel so *angry*. Why am I so angry? When did I come inside? I stop as I suck in a sharp breath, taking in the open front door—and the gun in my hand. *Where's the threat? Wasn't I outside?*

Wait.

Where's Emersyn?

"Oh no," I mumble, my hands shaking as my mind briefly flashing to her standing in my older brother's dusty room—the room I don't go in. "No, no, no." My eyes flicker back to the door.

Did Emersyn made a run for it?

Gunner bays so fucking loud that it pierces the rest of my insanity.

"What?!" I exasperate at him. "What am I supposed to do?" But he won't stop jumping at me, barking incessantly and running for the door, then back to me. I shake my head at him, frustrated. But after a few more times, I give in, knowing I have to face what I've done.

She's probably still alive. Maybe. Hopefully not. I'll have to explain now.

She doesn't know what she did, but she fucked up. That room is full of all the things that broke me. It started with my younger brother dying in action, then my parents dying in a car accident, and then... Thomas. *Fuck.* I swallow the grief tugging at me as I charge through the snow, ready to make peace with this shitty situation. I hate being reminded that I've buried *every single* one of my family members.

But only *one* was done by my own hand.

And Gunner is all I have left of him.

"Oh fuck," I groan, as I spot a flashlight amidst the clearing night. I never made it far in my search when I saw Tommy's room light come on.

Gunner's bark grows increasingly panicked, and I give him the track command. He's hesitant, but obeys, just like always.

Who the fuck is out here?

I move in silence, giving Gunner space to trail and committing myself to the task at hand rather than my short blackout. My dog falls into silence, tearing through the chest deep snow on his body.

I'll find you, Em. And then I'll fix this.

I trudge through the snow, following my dog, but with

every passing moment, I grow more concerned about the third human out in this snow. The beams of a flashlight have faded, meaning that someone is concealing themselves in the dark.

Maybe SAR?

I'm not sure if searchers would come looking for her right at the break. I think about her running out here in the cold, terrified. I feel sick with remorse, and sick that I'll have to tell her that I don't remember it.

Why am I like this? I want to fucking scream. *Why?*

Suddenly, I stop, standing in the snow. Maybe I should just let this happen. Whoever is out here, is probably better than me.

But... *what if they're not?*

That sends me forward again. All I want is to put her by the fire and tell her that I'm sorry for what I did—but it'll probably happen again.

Fuck, I hate me right now. She didn't know.

She didn't know not to go in that room.

This is my fault.

My boots crunch quietly through the snow, and then I spot the headlights of a Jeep parked on the other side of my gate. I grit my teeth and raise my rifle. I can't help it. With the crosshair on the headlight, I fire, killing the light. I repeat for the second and the fog lights.

Then, I listen, my keen ear picking up hushed whispers and...

The name Adam.

An ugly dose of envy pours through my veins. "Find

him," I growl to Gunner, and he kicks into high gear, baying out into the night in an eerie low hum. My pulse throbs in the side of my head, and I've now got tunnel vision on Em's ex-boyfriend. He had balls to show up here and I suddenly have someone *new* to blame.

And a trespasser.

CHAPTER 12

EMERSYN

"WHAT THE FUCK IS GOING ON?" Adam whispers to me as I grab his arm and drag him into a thicket of trees. His blond hair is tucked up under a beanie as he gives me a deplorable glare.

My heart pounds in the side of my head, terror sending a shiver down my spine. "You don't understand... The guy who lives here... He's not... *stable.*" I swallow hard as Adam's expression shifts, his hazel eyes widening. "I think he's going to kill us."

"*What?!*" Adam whisper yells as Gunner lets out a choppy bark.

I stifle a cry. "We're not going to be able to outrun him. There's no way. I don't... I don't understand him. But I think there's something wrong with him, and I think..." My voice trails off as I put it together. "I triggered him," I say softly.

"What the fuck did you do?" Adam snaps. "What did you do to piss him off?"

"I...I..." I can't bring myself to say anything to him as his gaze bores into me. My mind replays the heated kiss, the way I *wanted* Turner more than I ever wanted Adam in that way. "I just—"

Gunner bays, and I startle, realizing that he's a lot closer than before.

"I'll show the fucker," Adam growls, reaching into his coat pocket and pulling out a pistol. "He's not gonna get us, Em. I'll shoot them both."

I grab his hand, shaking my head. "I don't think you understand. Turner *won't* miss. He shot my phone out of my hand in the middle of the blizzard."

Adam curls his lip. "So you're on a first name basis with this guy, huh? Kind of weird for someone who shot at you. My guess is you've been doing more—"

"You're *really* going to point that out right now?" I exasperate, cutting him off. "I seriously thought the guy was easing up until... *this.*"

"Right," he snorts, racking the gun and peering out from behind one of the trees. I stand close to Adam, who I always thought was a bigger guy—but he's got nothing on Turner, who has to be three to four inches taller and wider. I wrap my arms around myself.

"Don't shoot the dog," I say quietly. "Please. It's not his faul—"

"Shut up," Adam growls. "We're getting out of here. Whatever it takes."

I swallow hard, the cold seeping deep beneath my parka,

chilling my bones. Tears brim my eyes, but for some reason, the feeling is a mixture of fear *and* grief for whatever is to come. I peer up into the starless sky, wondering if there's any way for this to end without bloodshed.

"So, your boyfriend is here, Em," Turner's graveled voice cuts through the night, echoing around us in a cold haunting tone. "Did you tell him what you did with me tonight? Before you went snooping though my house?"

"What's he talking about?" Adam looks back at me, confusion in his expression.

"It was nothing," I lie. "He's just—"

"What did *you do* with him?" Adam cuts me off, his voice breaking from a whisper. "Fuck him?"

"No, we just—we just kissed—"

"Oh for fuck's sake!" Adam roars at me. "I fucking *braved a blizzard* for you, and you were just fine, fucking some guy five seconds after we broke up. I knew you were like this. I *knew* it."

Guilt slams into my chest, and suddenly I feel horrible. "I'm so sorry. This has just been the weirdest—"

"Shut up," he seethes. "I know you're a fucking whore, Em. You probably fucked more guys while we were together."

"No, I didn't," I exasperate, my voice breaking with hurt. "I wouldn't ever—"

Gunner's violent bay cuts me off and he tears through the thicket, barreling toward us.

"Fucker!" Adam shouts, raising his pistol. He goes for

the trigger, and I shove his arm as it fires, the bullet burying into the ground. "What the fuck is wrong with you?" He yells at me as Gunner stands back a few feet, barking at us.

I open my mouth to say something, but the crack of a rifle silences me... And Adam instantly slumps to the ground, a clear hole right through his head. Crimson soaks the snow around him, and I stifle my scream, clamping my hand over my mouth. My vision grows blurry as I sink to my knees.

I'm next. I'm next.

I hear the crunch of boots in the snow and feel the hot breath of Gunner as he sniffs my head, as if he's trying to check on me. I cover my face with my hands, unable to look up as I feel the presence of Turner looming above me.

"You didn't even check him to make sure he was dead," Turner chuckles wickedly. "Some girlfriend you are, huh?"

My numb hands feel like ice sickles to my hot tears as I wait with bated breath, hearing Turner roll Adam's body. My stomach lurches violently as I steal a glance, Adam's face already blueish, his eyes wide with death. Bile shoots up the back of my throat, and I heave, vomiting into the snow.

"Must be your first dead body," he says flatly as he uses his boot to roll Adam back face down. "I'll have to get the tractor to deal with this—and the jeep. What a fucking mess." His tone is so eerily nonchalant that it feels unreal.

My heart pounds in my ears as I wait, my eyes squeezed shut and hidden in my hands again. Finally, I feel the barrel of the rifle dig into my upper back.

"Get up."

"Just get it over with," I scream out, finally getting the

nerve to look up at Turner. My eyes meet his, and there's *nothing* in the dark irises as they peer down at me. I suddenly hate every ounce of empathy I ever gave this man.

"Get. Up." He presses the barrel into my back with more force.

"No," I spit fire at him, my fear shifting to anger. "Just fucking *do* it, Turner."

His neck warmer is pulled up past his nose, but he jerks it down and then kneels to get eye level with me. He drops his rifle in the snow, and I attempt to shy away as his gloved fingers wrap around my jaw. My teeth chatter as he draws my face to his, our noses brushing, eyes locked—and *finally,* I see a flicker of something so painful, I have to look away.

"I don't *want* to kill you. If I wanted to, I would've by now." His voice is so quiet, I can barely make out his words.

Anger burns in my chest, and I can't hold back any longer. "Yeah? But from afar, right? Because you wouldn't have the fucking *balls* to look me in the eye when you put a bullet in my head."

His brows raise, and time seems to freeze for a moment, the two of us locked in that position. I swallow hard as his grip digs into my skin, and he then tips my head back. His gaze dropping to my lips. For a moment, I think he might kiss me.

But instead, he drops his hand away and rises. Turner picks up his rifle, slings it over his shoulder, and then disappears into the night, leaving me there. I brush my numb fingers across my jaw, still feeling a burning sensation from where his hand was. I eye the face-down dead body of my ex-boyfriend—who had come to rescue me.

I zone out, my eyes blurry with moisture.

And then it hits me.

He has a phone.

I crawl across the snow to his body, and then hesitate, the blood having melted the snow around him. I take a deep breath and then go for his pockets, fishing for *something.*

"You won't find his phone," I hear Turner from somewhere in the woods. "Or his gun."

Because you took it, I think glancing up through the trees in the direction of where Turner disappeared. I try to breathe as I stand wearily to my feet, Gunner still sitting and watching me with curiosity. My legs tremble as I wipe the fresh tears from my face.

Should I make a run for it? The thought crosses my mind as I watch the distance grow between Turner and me. Internally, I know that it's useless, but the desperation and...*anger* I feel toward Turner makes me want vengeance—or something. I don't even know *how* to reason with what just happened.

It was to protect Gunner, maybe. Big maybe.

I grit my teeth as I trudge in the direction of Turner, my fists clenched and Gunner following me closely. As I break from the trees, I see Adam's Jeep tearing through the now open gate. It's equipped with snow chains and clearly, Turner knows how to drive in the snow. He stops inside the gate, and goes back, shutting and locking it.

He doesn't even look in my direction as he climbs back in

my dead ex-boyfriend's car and roars past me, using acceleration and quick swerves to power around large drifts. I stand in knee deep snow, watching the Jeep until it disappears somewhere.

"What do I do?" I ask Gunner, batting away fresh tears. "I'm so fucked now."

Gunner tilts his head at me, and then bounds off in the direction of Turner. The dog has no idea how big of a monster his master is—and if he does, he doesn't care. My shoulders slump as I start after him, leaving Adam's body in the cold. My mind replays the moments before Adam was killed, and the mixed emotions that follow are almost as horrifying as the death itself.

Adam was never the *nicest* boyfriend, but he wasn't the worst, either. Sure, he got a little mouthy, but for fuck's sake, he didn't deserve to be shot in the head. He was doing his duty, coming to rescue me—and Turner *shot* him. My stomach lurches again as I crest the hill, seeing the barn door slid open. Turner hops in the Jeep and pulls into the barn.

And just like that, the Jeep is gone as soon as the door closes.

No one will find us out here.

I wrap my arms around myself as Turner steps through the walk-through door, freshly cleared. His face warmer is down around his neck, and at first, he doesn't notice me. His expression is almost...*grim*. He runs a hand down his face, and then notices me, hardening his gaze.

"Go inside." His words are eerily calm. In fact, he appears under the single pole light as fatigued as ever. "*Go,*" Turner repeats when I just stand there, watching him. His gesture toward the cabin gets me in motion. Every step feels heavy, numb, and I'm not sure if it's the shock or the cold.

Maybe both.

I don't say a word to him as I make my way to the cabin, lugging myself up the steps. I push open the door, the warmth burning my face. The scent of dinner still hangs in the air, and some soft tune still plays on my laptop. I let it keep playing as I shove off my shoes and head straight for the hearth.

Collapsing on the floor, I leave on my soaked jacket, jeans, and stare into the flames, licking up fresh heat—all the while Adam lays dead in the snow somewhere outside. I don't know what Turner's going to do with the body, but I hear a rumbling engine, reminding me of a tractor or some sort of equipment.

And then it hits me.

He could've dug me out with that... He could've let me go.

I squeeze my eyes shut as fresh tears spill down my cheeks, my nose and cheeks burning. Maybe the blizzard prevented him from letting me go, but now, there's a murder. I'm a witness.

I'm never making it out of here.

Resting my forehead against my wet knees, I let the sobs break free from my chest. I heard once that letting yourself cry is sometimes a relief. Well, right now, it doesn't feel like one to me. It only seems to emphasize the *shitty* cards I've been dealt. But still, I let myself cry so hard I can't breathe.

Until I hear the doorknob of the front door.

Then, I quiet myself, shutting down whatever feelings are beneath the surface. I don't want Turner to know a damn thing I feel. Ever again. He *almost* had me. He *almost* got invited inside my walls to know me.

But now, I'm locking myself away.

And I don't care if it gets me killed.

CHAPTER 13

TURNER

BURYING a body in frozen ground is a fucking task. I don't mark the guy's grave when I'm finished. He doesn't deserve it. I heard the way he spoke to Emersyn, and the way he went after my dog. On *my* property. Sure, it was the heat of the moment. Sure, I was trying to kill her five minutes prior in a blackout. But still. He had to go—and the blood spilled doesn't really bother me. Not so long as I can justify it.

"Looks like it'll be Christmas before the east sides of the county get cleared," the voice on the radio spits. *"Next round of snow is already here."*

I turn off the radio and leave it in the barn with the Jeep. I know I'll have to break the vehicle down and get rid of it. Or maybe drive it into the river when the freeze clears in the Spring. I'll figure it out. But not tonight. I need to get inside and check on Emersyn. She's pissed at me. Rightfully so, I suppose.

But at least she's not dead. She should be thankful for that. Maybe.

I make the journey back to the cabin just as the snow starts to fall again. I sigh, knowing that if we get another few feet of snow, things are going to be even more complicated—and that's more time in enclosed spaces. I push away the thought as I open the front door, spotting Emersyn by the fire, her head down.

She's still in her parka and drenched jeans. My chest tightens at the sight. It's a lot worse than I expected. For some reason, I didn't think about the repercussions of killing her boyfriend. Er, ex-boyfriend. Whatever he was. He thought he was doing her a favor by rescuing her. But it was his fucking duty. He shouldn't have complained about it, called her a whore, or tried to kill my fucking dog—my only lifeline.

"You need to get out of those wet clothes," I say finally as I slide out of my snow pants and parka. I expect her to rattle off some sort of snarky reply.

But she doesn't. She acts like she doesn't even hear me.

"I *said,* you need to get out of those clothes and get some sleep."

Emersyn lifts her head but doesn't look at me. Her eyes stay focused on the flames in front of her as she slides out of the parka. She then slowly rises to her feet, her coat in her arms. I walk to her, and she remains unmoved as I take it from her arms.

"I'll hang this up for you."

Nothing in response.

Emersyn turns on her heels and heads down the hallway, her jeans sticking to her as she slips away into the darkness.

"Goodnight," I call after her, my stomach swirling.

Maybe I should've killed her.

Because this fucking feeling I have now, is *killing* me.

FOUR BLIZZARD DAYS PASS. *Four.* Emersyn won't look me in the face. She won't utter a *word* to me. She went from talking to fill the silence to forcing me to drown in it. She eats granola bars and stays in the bedroom. I only know she's here by the fucking lump in the bed when I pass through to piss or shower.

And I'm not okay with this arrangement.

I tried to give her space, but tonight, I'm done with it. She's either going to talk to me, or she's going to fucking die at my dinner table. She will *not* be a fucking ghost in my house.

I set dinner, another shit casserole, on the table, and then decide to *force* her to sit at my fucking table. I rap my fist on the bedroom door. "Dinner."

Nothing.

I reach for the knob, and turn it, shoving the door open with force. "I *said*, it's *dinner time.*"

She sits cross-legged on the bed, her damp hair spilling over her shoulders, and her black sweatshirt hanging loosely on her shrinking frame. She stares at her hands.

"Get up," I command, taking a step toward her. "You're eating with me tonight."

"No," she says, her voice barely audible.

"Yes, you are," I stalk toward her, catching the lavender scent of her as I come within a foot of where she sits. "You *are* going to eat with me."

She shakes her head.

"Fuck, Emersyn," I seethe, clenching my fists. "Get up."

"No," she answers. Rage floods my vision, and I don't know if I want to fall to my fucking knees and *beg* her to come with me or choke the life right out of her. *Why is she doing this? Why does this all have to be so hard?*

I reach down, clamping my hand around her forearm. "*You're coming.*" I drag her off the side of the bed, and she whimpers as I give her zero gentleness. "You're making me do it this way. I won't let you die of starvation."

She stays silent as I damn near drag her the entire way to the kitchen. I pull out the chair, force her to sit down, and then fill her plate with a chicken rice casserole. She goes to stand up, but I'm faster, pulling my pistol and setting it beside my dinner plate. She sits back down.

"That's what I fucking thought," I mutter. "You want to give me the silent treatment, but you still don't want to die."

She lifts her eyes to me then, meeting my gaze for the first time in four days. "I'd really just hate for you to get blood in your food."

"I'd eat it anyway," I snarl back at her disgusted expression.

"Sick fuck." She shakes her head, stabbing a piece of

chicken with her fork. She lifts it up, like she might take a bite, but then sets it back down.

I take her in, sitting under the warm glow of the kitchen light for the first time since I killed her boyfriend, and it fucking *hurts*. I barely know this woman, really, but yet I hate myself for being the reason she looks so...*fucked up*. Dark circles hold her jade eyes, dulled and puffy. Her lips are cracked. Her hair disheveled. She doesn't look like the woman that danced with me in the kitchen four days ago.

She looks like walking death.

And *I* did it. She's starting to look like Thomas did. Maybe it's better when people don't survive me long.

I force myself to eat, now me being the one who can't look *her* in the face. I've taken a lot of lives, but this is the first time I've seen the repercussions in person—the damage I've done. The person I killed is dead in the ground, at peace, but this woman... She's in hell right now.

I need a drink. I scoot back from the table, suddenly sick with myself for making her eat at my table. I go to the liquor cabinet, something I don't frequent, grabbing a bottle of bourbon. I pour myself a glass, and then down the whole thing.

Maybe I should kill her. That would bring her peace.

But I hate the idea. I hate the idea of her being with *him*, even in death. I'm sure that makes me a sick fucking bastard. I didn't want her here. But now that she is... I glance back to her, meeting those somber fucking eyes.

I want the Em back that I kissed.

What do I have to do? Do I have to tell her the truth about me? I want to tell her everything, and my expression must give me away, because for a split second, there's curiosity in her face instead of coldness. I look away.

"It's the winter solstice," I grunt, pouring myself another glass. "Four days until Christmas."

"Why'd you do it?" Her question cuts through my walls, slicing into me. "Turner," she repeats herself after a few long beats of silence. "Why did you kill him?"

I blow out a breath. I can answer this. "He tried to kill Gunner. I need Gunner."

She lets out a sharp breath of annoyance, like she can't argue with that. "Okay, but then why did you try to kill me?"

I look up as I tip the glass back, knowing this one is going to lead to a spiral of truth. "You were in my older brother's room."

"I didn't know the room was off-limits," she says quietly. "I started looking around when I shouldn't have, but... I just wanted to know you."

I swallow the lump growing in my throat. "You don't want to know me, Em. There's nothing good left of me."

"Yeah, I was stupid," she mumbles, surprising me by not asking anymore questions. She scoots back from the table, leaving her plate basically untouched. "And now, I'd rather die not knowing you." A tear rolls down her cheek as she stands to her feet. She doesn't wipe it away, leaving it to taunt me, reminding me of just how horrible I really am.

She goes to walk past me, and I panic, my hand landing on her bicep. "Don't go back there. Just stay. Please."

"Why?" Emersyn tips her head back. "So you can try to

intimidate me with your guns and psychosis? You don't scare me anymore, Turner." The numbness in her face is gut wrenching.

"I don't want to scare you, Em," I blurt out, my guard slipping in desperation. "I just want you to stay here with me. I have a TV. I can hook it up for you. We could watch a movie. I can—"

"Shut up," she cuts me off, her voice painfully soft. "I don't want your niceties. I don't want your fucking TV or your time. I want you to decide what you're going to do with me, and just fucking *do it.*"

I down the rest of my bourbon and set the glass on the counter, and then jerk her body into mine. She lets out a sharp breath, and I back her into the cabinet. I grab her chin and force her to look at me.

"What if *this* is what I want to do with you?" I lean down, my nose brushing hers.

"So you want to play house then, Turner?" she spews back at me, her voice cold. "Might as well kill me, stuff me, and then set me at your table. You'll get more of a reaction from my dead body than living."

I grit my teeth, trying to keep my anger at bay as Gunner whines from somewhere. "Do you just *want* me to kill you? Because trust me, when I blackout again, I *will.*"

She *spits* in my face. "Go ahead. Saves me the agony of living with you, you sick fucking psycho." If she means to anger me, it doesn't work. It doesn't enrage me in the slightest. Instead, it drains me of emotion leaving my stomach feeling nauseous and my chest tight. I release her, backing away.

She finally sees me for who I am, no sugarcoating it to herself. There's not an ounce of denial. It is what it is—and it fucking *hurts*.

CHAPTER 14

EMERSYN

THE SNOW FINALLY BREAKS, but it doesn't mean the same as it did before. All it means now is that the sun beams through the window, taunting me with a freedom I know I'll never have. I slide into a pair of dark wash jeans and an olive colored sweatshirt, pull my hair up into a messy bun, and step out of the bedroom. Part of me hopes Turner is still upstairs with his bourbon—the way he left yesterday evening.

But there's this unwanted *small* part of me that hopes I'll run into him.

I hate that part of me. It's the same part that made me feel guilty for spitting in his face, which had the opposite effect of what I thought it would. I *hurt* him, which is maybe what I wanted. But two wrongs don't make a right, right? I don't know anymore.

"I'm going outside to get started clearing," Turner tells

me as soon as I appear at the end of the hallway. Gunner stands beside him, wagging his tail. I nod, meeting his eyes. He instantly looks away. It's like a game.

And now he's the one who won't face me.

"How much snow?"

"Four days' worth," he grunts, opening the backdoor and disappearing. I watch him go, the door slamming shut behind him. I stare after him, wondering why I still feel the urge to follow him. I suppressed it, but it's still there. I let out a sigh, my stomach growling. Slowly, my appetite has resurfaced, and honestly, the grief has faded astronomically faster than I expected.

In fact, I think there might be something wrong with me. But maybe this is just how I cope.

I shudder, and then grab a granola bar, spinning on my heels and heading back down the hallway. However, as I reach the end of the hallway, I make a right, heading up the stairs. Turner is going to be out a while, and as I peer out the window, I see him already shoveling snow around the house.

"I lied to you," I say, watching him through the window. "I *do* want to know who's going to try and kill me." There's a knot in my throat as the words leave my lips, and I'm almost certain it makes me crazy.

But if I *know* him, maybe I stand a chance to survive him.

I head straight for the room he found me in, slipping inside. I leave the lights off, letting the natural light fill the room, and I shut myself in. I should hear him come in, but if I don't, I'll at least have a chance to hide. It's a shitty plan, but I *have* to know why Turner did what he did—and I have a good feeling this room means something.

As soon as I click the door shut, I head for the desk in the corner. I pick up the top letter first, which is an explanation that he's not eligible to receive disability with a dishonorable discharge. I set that to the side, picking up a handwritten letter from someone named Calvin Bradford. It's handwritten, worn, and it appears it's been poured over more times than once, dated December 11, 2013.

Thomas,

Thank you for reaching out. I won't be stateside for another six months. When I am, I will give you a call and see how things are going. I don't want to leave you without more information, however. I know you have the official documents, but you deserve the off-record truth, too.

Your brother is struggling with severe PTSD, but I believe it's developing into more. His outbursts are violent, and even though they follow with heartbreaking remorse for his actions, I believe that he's going to need significant clinical help to get past his blackouts that have developed. He nearly killed me, and his psychologist could only explain it as a break in his psyche. I don't think it's a high or addiction. It's the trauma eating him alive. I'm worried one day, he will snap and hurt someone he loves.

I'm not angry at him for what happened. He was one of the best in his unit. Don't ever let his mental illness overshadow his bravery for the duration of his enlistment. I did everything I could for a medical discharge, but unfortunately, it didn't come to pass. Just don't forget he saved eight men. They have not forgotten him.

He suffered a great loss with Taylor passing and you all's parents a month later in the accident a little over two years ago. I believe he stuck it out and served for another year after, because he thought going through the motions would fix him— but I think it only prolonged the buildup and then the break.

But it's just a theory, Thomas. I don't know if that's what's going on. I just know, no one should lose their parents and brother in a month span. I wish every day the car accident wouldn't have happened. I'm so incredibly sorry for you and Turner's losses. Don't give up on him but please keep your safety in mind.

Give him my regards. He has my phone number. If he wants my help, call me. He hasn't responded to anything I've sent him thus far. I know he is in a dark place. I hope he finds his way out someday.

Bradford

I blink away the tears as I set the letter back down on the desk, my heart aching with sympathy. Turner killed Adam, but for fuck's sake, how much can one man go through? I then begin to open drawers, finding mostly irrelevant papers, other than some still full prescriptions issued by psychiatrists. When I finally make it to the final drawer, I find a journal. I flip it open, seeing Thomas's name.

It starts August 1st 2011, and I start flipping through it, noting that Thomas is working on the cabin, planning a hunting trip for him, his father, Turner, and their brother, Taylor, when they're home later that year. I take a seat in the floor, sitting cross legged as I keep reading, stopping on the ones that mention Turner.

September 1, 2011

Turner and Taylor were deployed on a mission. No idea where they went. Praying for their safe return.

September 28, 2011

Still haven't heard from Turner or Taylor. I have a bad feeling in my gut. Pops called, wanting to know if I'd heard from him. I told him no but didn't express my worry.

October 5, 2011

Turner said their mission was supposed to last a few weeks. It's been a month. Still trying not to worry.

October 15, 2011

Finally heard from Turner. Taylor was killed three days ago. No details. I can't believe it. Turner will be home in a few days.

October 18, 2011

I picked up Turner today. Something isn't right. He's not himself. He's torn up over Taylor. They were in combat, providing rescue aid. He said, 'they got into bad shit.' That's all I know. His commanding officer said he is being nominated for a medal of honor. Turner doesn't appear to care. I'm worried about him, but I know he's grieving.

October 20, 2011

Turner, Pops, and I went out to the range today. It didn't go well. Turner seemed to have some kind of flashback. Pops talked him out of it. He goes back in a couple of weeks. I hope he gets some help.

October 25, 2011

Taylor's services were today. Turner handled it better than I expected. I miss my brother, but I'm thankful Turner made it back.

October 27, 2011

I can't believe I'm writing this. Mom and Pops are gone. This might be the worst day of my life. Turner is so sick. He needs help. He was at the store and had another flashback. He barricaded himself in the bathroom. Mom and Pops were on their way to help him when a fucking box truck ran a red light. I couldn't be in two places at once. I left the Marines to retrieve Turner. They said he'll get the help he needs. I am glad I got to say goodbye to Mom and Pops at the hospital. They said not to be mad at Turner. I'm not. I swear I'm not. But fuck, I'm trying so hard not to hate him.

I pause from reading, my stomach sick and heart breaking. I use my sleeve to dab away the tears as I continue. The mentions of Turner fade for next year, only stating that he's getting help and staying in the service. The two aren't talking at that point. It's not until late 2012 they start again.

December 14, 2012

Turner was awarded the medal of honor tonight. Proud of him. But he didn't look good. I should talk to him more.

December 20, 2012

I had to pick up Turner today. He is being discharged. He is still sick. I don't think they fixed him. He brutally attacked his commanding officer. Somehow, they've managed not to press charges. I don't understand, but I got him and brought him to the cabin. We're all we have. I feel guilty. I wasn't there for him. I'll be there for him now. I swear.

January 18, 2013

He doesn't sleep. He paces. He shouts. He's messed up in the head. I'm too tired to even write about him. I'm doing everything I can. I swear. I'm taking him to all the specialists. I don't know what else to do.

March 15, 2013

I'm running out of options. Turner seems to just go dead, and he starts playing war. He flies off the handle and goes for whatever is closest. Then he cries. For days. God something is so wrong, but I don't know what to do. Why aren't these doctor's helping him? I've made a call to someone out of state, hoping someone will help me help him.

June 29, 2013

He's getting better, I think. No outbursts since he started therapy sessions with this new doctor. He tells me he still struggles. He says he can't help it. Everything goes dark in his head. I don't understand that, but I hope in time, he can work out of it. I got him a PTSD dog today. Turner named him Gunner.

July 5, 2013

He made it through the fireworks. I'm so proud of him. We're really getting somewhere.

October 12, 2013

Two years without Taylor. Turner had a bad day today, but he's okay. He has Gunner.

October 30, 2013

Things feel like they're on the right track. He's doing great. I think we're going to a Halloween party tomorrow. It'll be good for him.

November 1, 2013

Bad idea. He got into a fight and nearly beat some guy to death. I got him out of there. He left with his rifle this morning, and I don't know where he went. I know I should go look for him, but he had that dead look in his eyes. I hate to admit that it scares me.

November 23, 2013

Things are okay again. He seems antsy. I sent word to Bradford. I want him to have a good life.

December 24, 2013

His emotions are all over the place. Gunner keeps alerting to an episode. But I don't understand. He seems lucid. I can't tell. I'm starting to lose hope. I think my brother is permanently broken. I don't know what to do, but I think it's too much for me to handle anymore. He's going to hurt someone or a whole lot of people. I love him so much, but until he'll go somewhere to get help, I have to give up. He won't leave this cabin. It's like he wants to force himself to be tortured over and over. I need a break.

I shut the book as I finish the last entry and put it back in a daze. Where is Thomas now? Did he take a break and never come back? I stand to my feet, feeling an overwhelming mixture of emotions. All of that took place over ten years ago. A decade. Isn't that how long it had been since Turner listened to music?

The story starts to mesh together in my mind as I slip out of the room undetected, padding down the stairs and slipping into my hiking boots. His younger brother died in action, his parents died in a car accident a month later, a year after that, Turner was discharged, and then... *Where's Thomas now? Did he abandon Turner?*

I sigh, raking my fingers through my hair. If Thomas managed to get out of here, I can, too. I take a deep breath and get dressed to head outside. The entries have made me more curious than ever, and I just...

I need to make nice, so I can escape.

CHAPTER 15

TURNER

I STAB the shovel in the snow, huffing as I take in what progress I've made. Once I clear the way, I can get the tractor out and start really making some progress. My eyes cast across the backyard, and then to the hill a little bit further out. I can't see the cross, but I know it's there. The anniversary of eleven years is in just three days.

And so is Christmas.

"Hey," a voice startles me, I whip my head to see Emersyn, standing about ten feet from me in the path I've cleared. "Do you need some help?" I stare at her, trying to process the fact she's talking to me on her own free will. "Do you need some water or something?"

I shake my head slowly. "No, I'm good."

She drops my gaze, her eyes falling to her boots and then rising to meet mine again. "I'm sorry for being such a jerk to you last night."

"What?" I raise my brows, shocked.

She takes a step forward, her face full of emotion—that I don't quite understand. "I'm sorry, Turner. I didn't...I think I now understand that..." Her voice trails off, and I get what she's trying to say.

"That there's something wrong with me," I finish for her. "You must've taken another trip upstairs." Irritation and anger flood my system, but the embarrassment is far greater. "It's fine." She takes another step toward me, and I take one back away from her, halfway expecting her to pull a fucking gun on me or something. She's loaded with the ability to destroy me.

And now, I'm the one who's scared.

"Turner..." She keeps encroaching, finally stopping right in front of me. "Why didn't you kill me when you killed Adam? Or when we were up in the room? I know about the whole... *blackout* thing."

"I don't know about up in Thomas's room. But I was present when I killed Adam, and I didn't kill you because I want you too much." The truth slips from my lips unfiltered, and I know now this woman is going to be my downfall. She's too intrigued for her own good, and now, she's made the bold move of putting her hand on my chest...

And her mouth on mine.

I fall into her intoxicating kiss, threading my fingers through her hair and knocking her hood out of her face. My tongue dances across hers, tasting the mint on her tongue. She came out here wanting this to happen... and it's such a turn on. For a moment, I let myself believe she wants me just as fucking bad as I want her.

I lift her into the air, wrapping her legs around me as I rip open the walk-through door of the barn, shutting it behind us with my heel. Heading straight to my workbench, I clear it in one swoop, sitting her down and tearing at her jeans. I'm going to make this woman *mine,* if only in my head.

"It's freezing," Emersyn pants as I wriggle her out of her jeans and boots. "We can go inside..."

"No," I growl. "You're not getting the chance to change your fucking mind this time."

She shivers against me, now bare from the waist down. The heater is running, but there's no escaping the chill in the air. I take her mouth again while I undo my pants, feeling the hesitancy in her kiss. My mind kicks into gear.

She's just fucking you because she feels sorry for you.

I grit my teeth at the intrusive thought, knowing more than likely that's the case—but I don't care. I'm desperate the way she made me feel in the kitchen when we danced. I trail away from her mouth as I drag her forward, and right onto my cock. A burst of fucking pleasure erupts in the form of a groan, years of abstinence dissipating as her wet walls grip me.

"Holy shit," I erupt, buring myself in her. She sucks in a sharp breath, her nails finding the back of my neck and digging in. I kiss her neck as her head tips back, an aroused moan slipping from her throat.

She rocks against me, grinding against my body. I bite

down on her neck, and she cries out, her pussy tightening around me. I grip her bare ass, as I start to pound into her, chasing a high I haven't felt in so long—or maybe ever.

"*Turner*," Em moans out my name as she bounces against me, her hips rocking as she grinds herself against me every time.

I'm buried all the way in her, as far as I can physically go, and it still isn't enough. "You're heaven," I groan, my release already building. It's been too long since I've had sex. I explode inside of her, gasping at the thick pleasure that's been absent for so long.

You're mine now, Em.

I pull out of her, and then drop to my knees.

"What are you doing?" Her eyes widen as my mouth connects with her inner thigh. "You don't have to—" My tongue gliding through her slit silences her mid-sentence, and she breaks out in a whimper.

"You taste better than I imagined," I rasp, a tinge of myself mixed with her. That's how it should be. She should always be full of me. I've never been possessive with a woman before, but I didn't know Emersyn then.

If only I met her before I got fucked in the head.

I push the thought away, sucking her into my mouth and running my tongue over her clit. She cries out, her eyes closing as her fingers glide through my hair. She squirms against me, and I pick up my pace, taking her all the way to the edge.

"*Turner...*" she moans out as she explodes, her orgasm tensing her legs around my head. I grow rigid again at the sultry tone of her voice, and I stroke myself as I lap up the mixture of her and me. Her breaths are ragged as I rise to my feet, and then reach for her, dragging her off the table.

"What're you doing?" she squeals as she drops to her feet, surprise in her eyes.

"I'm not done," I rumble, spinning her around. I bend her over, taking in her perky ass. I land a hard slap, and then push back into her.

"*Oh,*" she pants at the new angle, bracing against the workbench. I grip her waist, and leverage against her, jerking her body back and forth against mine. A renewed sense of self floods my body, and the high this woman brings is more exhilarating than anything I've felt in years.

And now, I *know* I won't regret this moment.

I fuck her until she's crying my name over and over, her pussy raw and swollen. I come with force, exploding with a groan as I unload for a second time. I catch my breath as I come down from the high, collapsing over her and planting a kiss on her shoulder.

"I've been wanting to do that since you showed up here," I admit, resting my head against her just long enough to take one more breath. I push off her then, taking in the sight of her cum-slick pussy and spread legs. Shakily, she straightens, wincing as she goes for her clothes. Grief fills my chest as she slowly wriggles into the bootcut jeans.

"I'm sorry for hurting you," I say, taking a step forward and buttoning her jeans for her.

"You can apologize when I'm not walking right in the

morning," she laughs, but then it fades when she meets my gaze.

"Not that kind of hurt," I clarify, though I wish that's all it was. "Your boyfriend was an asshole though—not that I'm much better. But I'm not sorry he's dead. I'm *just* sorry I hurt you."

"It's okay." Her eyes flicker with something I don't pick up entirely, and I drop my hand as my instincts kick in. She looks past me to the Jeep parked at the back of my shop.

What's she thinking? Something doesn't set right with me, but I don't press. "Why don't you go inside? It's cold out here."

She furrows her brow, disappointment written in her expression. "Are you staying out here?"

I nod. "For now. I need to clear as much as I can."

"What're you going to do with that?" She blurts out, pointing to the Jeep.

"Uh," I rub the back of my neck. "I'm not sure yet." I don't like feeling like telling her that it's not the first vehicle I've ever had to dispose of. She *thinks* she's got me figured out by the documents and letters she found in my brother's room. She has no idea what happened on Christmas.

The history in that room stopped being recorded eleven years ago. I can guarantee, if she had any clue of the sin I committed against my own brother, she wouldn't be so willing to spread her legs for me.

The demons in me don't discriminate between the people I love and the people I don't. It's just whatever warm body is in the way, and while she's seen me act out of calculated anger...

She hasn't met my inner monster fully. And if she stays, I know she will.

I sigh as she walks away. *What the hell am I supposed to do?* If I let her go, she'll go to the police about Adam. If I keep her here, she'll end up buried next to my brother... Is there any way out of this?

CHAPTER 16

EMERSYN

It's since gone dark outside, and Turner still hasn't come in. I'm not sure if what happened between us is the reason—and I did something wrong—or if it's entirely unrelated. When the moment started, I thought of it as survival. When it ended, I wanted more of him.

Why do I still *have a soft spot for him?* I flip back the covers and crawl into bed, mulling it over and wincing at the ache between my legs. His story is so freaking sad, and maybe that's where my empathy comes from—but also, I'm *trapped* here. He's tried to kill me. He murdered Adam.

But maybe it's part of his mental health issues?

I snort. All murderers have mental health issues, and I don't feel sorry for most of them. I turn over onto my stomach and bury my face in the pillow, letting out a frustrated sigh. It shouldn't feel this complicated, but then again, it was complicated between us long before he killed Adam and I willingly spread my legs for him.

It's out of survival. That's it. That's all it is.

But as I hear the cabin door creak open and Turner and Gunner step inside, my heart skips a beat—and my thighs clench. I lay there in silence for the next thirty minutes, waiting for what he's going to do next. Finally, the bedroom door creaks open, and I brace, waiting.

Once the shower starts, I roll over onto my side, facing the wall. This bedroom is about as bare as they come, furnished with just a queen-sized bed, one nightstand and a dresser. It reminds me of a hotel, except the bed feels more broken in, the sheets are flannel, and there's not one single piece of art on the wall—not even the shitty kind.

I close my eyes, willing myself to just fall asleep. I mean, the best way to die would probably be in my sleep, if he's going to kill me, right? Wrapping my arms around my body, I listen to the water shut off, Turner's footsteps creaking across the floor, and then a dresser drawer opening.

He's gone through these motions before with me in bed, and then he always leaves, disappearing somewhere upstairs... But not tonight. I feel him lingering, and the heat of his gaze burns into my body, heat flickering through my core. I swallow my nerves, waiting for his next move.

"I know you're not sleeping," he says, rustling with the covers on the opposite side of the bed. "You're holding your breath. What for?"

Heat creeps into my face. *How the hell does he know? How often has he watched me sleep?* I choose silence, and he lets out a sigh, crawling into bed beside me. The heat from his body is a nice touch, given the cold nights I've spent alone, and I have to physically force myself to stay put, rather than move toward him.

"So we're back to silence now?" His voice is flat, but there's a hint of emotion there—enough to cause me to roll over and face him, taking in the way he's lying on his back, his hand pressed against his forehead.

"No, we're not. I just don't know what to say."

He cocks his head in my direction, and even in the dark, I can make out his eyes focused on mine. "When you got here, you had a lot to say. All the time. I'm sorry I fucked that up for you."

Why is he suddenly acting like a decent person? I take a deep breath, the scenes in the kitchen of us dancing coming back to mind. Emotions bubble up in my chest, and I squeeze my eyes shut. "It's fine."

"It's not." His fingers brush my hair out of my face, sending tingles through my body and consequently relaxing me more than a murderer should. It's so hard to hate him, especially knowing so much about him. I slide my hand over his, where it's resting against my cheek, and breathe in, the woodsy masculine scent of him strangely comforting. He scoots closer, his legs brushing mine.

My eyes flutter open. "Why am I not scared of you, Turner?"

"I don't know." He searches my face. "But I liked you better when you were."

I frown. "Why?"

"Because now, even though you let me fuck you, you're indifferent. Maybe pissed. Sickened. It's all of the things that

I don't want you to feel toward me. Fear can be exhilarating, and I can turn it into excitement for you..." His voice trails off. "But I can't change you thinking I'm a sick fuck."

A knot grows in my throat, surprising remorse funneling in my chest. "I shouldn't have said that to you. I'm sorry. I didn't know..."

"No, I killed your boyfriend because I wanted to. He was a prick, and in the five seconds, I heard him speak, I knew he didn't understand what he had. So, I'm not sorry for it. I'm only sorry that I hurt you. I think that qualifies as a sick fuck."

I purse my lips, trying to process everything he's saying to me—and why the hell it makes me feel so warm and fuzzy inside. "Okay," I force the word out.

He chuckles quietly, removing his hand and rolling onto his back again. "Goodnight, Em."

I lay there in silence for a few moments, and then reach for him, giving into the part of me that wants him—the part of me that started out small and seems to be slowly taking over. He catches his breath as I draw myself into him, snuggling up to his body. Turner wraps his arm around me, holding me tightly.

"I don't hate you," I whisper to him, letting the warmth of his body and thud of his heartbeat lull me to sleep.

I FEEL him leave the bed early in the morning, and I scoot into the spot he was sleeping in, soaking in the heat until it grows cold. After laying there for a few minutes longer, I flip the forest green quilt back, giving up on getting anymore sleep.

I slide into a pair of light wash jeans and black sweatshirt, then brush my teeth and redo my messy bun. It's two days till Christmas, and it doesn't feel any different than any other day—not that it should. Guilt hits my chest as I think of Aaron and Catie, who have no idea that Adam is gone. Not to mention, my whole freaking family is probably worried sick about me. My stomach lurches, and I vomit into the toilet, losing what little I've eaten in the last few days.

"Oh hell, are you okay?" I feel a hand on my back as I heave again, the soreness between my legs emphasized as my thighs clench to steady myself. "What's wrong?"

I shake my head as I straighten, eyeing Turner wearily. "I'm fine," I choke out, wiping the tears away as I grab for a piece of toilet paper to wipe the corners of my mouth.

"Would you stop lying?" he snaps at me as I flush the toilet. "It's getting really old. You came out yesterday, playing some kind of horny empath, but now you're hurling your guts up? You're still not talking to me the way you did before, either," he exasperates, starting the sink and grabbing a cup for me to rinse my mouth out with.

"What do you expect?" I fire off back at him, losing my filter. "You fucking murdered someone *right* in front of me —and that guy, he has a fucking family and people who care about him. They're getting a dead brother and son for Christmas this year. Actually, worse. Because you know what? He's just going to fucking *disappear*, Turner, and you're not even sorry about it. Not to mention, a lesser offense, my family is probably worried sick about me."

His muscles visibly tense beneath his gray henley. "Yeah, you're right, and they can all join the rest of the world that doesn't have answers."

"Why?" I throw my hands in the air. "Why add to that? Isn't the world fucked up enough as it is? You could've let him go. You could've just told him to leave."

"He was a dick," Turner snaps at me. "He had it coming, and he tried to hurt my dog. You don't understand how much I *need* him."

"Maybe," I admit, meeting his gaze. "But let nature take its course. It's not your job to play judge and jury."

"No," he growls, suddenly angry. "I *will* play judge and jury in my house, on my fucking land. He chose to trespass and try to take away what's mine. *You*," he grabs my chin and hauls me to him, "are *mine*."

"You wish," I sneer, not backing down from the challenge. "You're not the only one who can shoot a gun in this house."

A wicked smile stretches across Turner's face as he pins me against the bathroom counter, his erection digging into my lower stomach. "You *really* know how to turn me on, Em. You better watch your mouth before I show you who's boss here." I *hate* the way I react to him, my body suddenly arguing with my senses. My chest heaves as he brushes his nose against mine. "Why did you let me have you, Em? If you think what I did was so bad?"

I open my mouth, but he continues. "You can tell me it's

self-preservation, but we both know, you were wet with anticipation for me." Turner's lips graze my skin as he makes it to my ear. "Maybe I'm not the only one here that has a jet-black heart, because whether you want to admit or not, you'd fuck me again right now. So maybe the fact that I'm a *sick fuck*, only arouses you more."

"Fuck you," I choke out, my underwear soaked with the evidence that he's *right*.

He breathes in deep, his exhale setting my skin fire. "Wouldn't you like to, Emersyn. But I have things to do. So be a good girl, and don't think about starting a war with me. I *always* win." He releases me then, and begins to walk away, leaving my heart thrumming in my ears.

"Turner," I grab his arm, tugging him back to me, breathless. "You can't win."

His jaw tenses, his eyes darkening. "And why is that, Em?"

I brush my fingertips across his cheek, swallowing the lump in my throat. "Because I'm already on your side, even if I don't know that I want to be."

Turner's eyes drop from mine, and he shakes his head, before slipping out of the bathroom and leaving me there in a stupor. I *just* admitted the truth I've been battling since everything happened...

And he didn't say a word.

Chapter 17

Turner

She meant it.

In all the toxic shit that's happened between us, I *know* she meant those words. Maybe she had ulterior motive at the beginning. Maybe when she fucked me, she did, too. But that? That was real...

And now she deserves the truth.

Maybe I can find a way to save her. I bite down on my lip as I start pulling on my snow pants and parka, Gunner bouncing around me. I don't want to kill her. That's been clear since day one. She might *actually* be capable of being here with me—maybe even loving me. Maybe we could have some sort of fucked up happy ending...

If I can just control myself.

And that's what I think about as I head out to my shop, thinking about Christmas. Could I win her over entirely? I eye the blocks of cedar in the corner when I enter, and my set of whittling knives. I used to make shit to pass the time. I head for it and take a seat at the bench, grabbing a small piece of wood and letting my hands begin to move. My mind empties of thoughts, and I lose myself for a while.

Hours later, I stare down at the wooden heart shaped pendent I've finished. It's not much, but really, I don't have much to give her anyway. I have plenty of money from inheritance, but I don't buy shit. It's nothing like what I'm sure her fancy ex-boyfriend would've gotten her.

I set it down on the workbench, and as I do, I hear the sound of metal on wood, the echo clapping into the midday. I jump out of my seat, shoving the heart in my inner jacket pocket and rush out of the barn.

Squinting into the clearing behind the house, I spot Gunner, his tail wagging as he watches Em, swinging an axe at a small tree. *What the hell is she doing? That's horrible firewood material, and I already cut enough for a few months.*

Shaking my head, I start toward her, thankful that I used the tractor to clear a lot of the snow away—minus digging out her truck. It's still partially covered, and I probably should uncover it, but it's the last thing on my list. She hasn't asked and I can't let her leave, either.

I don't know if I'll ever let her leave.

Em's shoulder drops with defeat as she stares at the maybe six-foot pine tree. She eyes me wearily as I approach. "I don't want your help."

"Don't waste this thing on firewood," I tell her, chuckling. "Let it grow."

She furrows her brow. "It's not for firewood. It's a Christmas tree. I just thought... I don't know." Em drops the axe in the snow as her cheeks flush an even deeper shade of red. "I don't even know how to do a real Christmas tree anyway."

"Here," I pick up the axe. If she wants a stupid fire hazard in the cabin, I'll give it to her. I swing the axe, and in two blows, have the little flimsy thing down. She watches me with wide eyes as I hold the axe back out to her. "Don't take any swings at me, and I'll dig out the shit to set this up inside."

She *actually* smiles, her black gloves wrapping around the wooden handle. "Deal."

I push away the memories that begin to creep in, as I drag the tree behind me to ready it. It's been fifteen years since I've had a Christmas tree, and with it comes the memories, back when I was fucking normal. When, if I got the chance to be home, I was surrounded by my mom's Christmas cooking, and my pop's laughter.

And Tommy.

And Taylor.

"Fuck," I mutter under my breath as I shove the barn door open, shaking my head as my hands tremble. This is why I avoid the holidays. It's a reminder of all the ways I fucked up. I drop the tree at the door, and head to the storage loft at the back, climbing the old wooden ladder. It creaks under my weight, and part of me wishes it would just fucking collapse.

But no, I make it up to the top, and take in all the painful shit—the family keepsake boxes, my father's hunting gear, my brother's military uniform, and the list could go on. I deserve to have to see the reminders of the mess I made. I take a deep breath, my head uneven and light as I slip past to the old Christmas tree stand of Tommy's when he lived here. I don't know who he put a Christmas tree up for.

But whatever.

I grab it, knowing that the last person to touch the metal was my dead brother. My stomach churns with remorse, flashbacks threatening. "Gunner," I call for my dog, clambering down the ladder. My head starts to pound at the speed of helicopter blades. "Gunner," I shout, the sounds of war fading in over the ringing in my ears.

Gunner's clumsy steps turn frantic as he rushes me, just in time for me to drop the stupid tree stand and latch onto him. I squeeze my eyes shut as the chaos of war erupts in my mind. Dread hangs heavy on my shoulders, and I breathe in evenly, counting to seven with every inhale and exhale. Fear penetrates my entire body, rolling over me and tempting a burst of adrenaline—the same adrenaline that awakens the war-chasing, murder hungry monster in me.

'You gotta go,' Taylor screams in my ear, as his heavy hand lands on the back of my neck. 'Get 'em out of here.'

"I'm not leaving you," I shout at him. "I'm not leaving you."

But Taylor doesn't say anything back. Warm, sticky liquid splatters across my neck as he spews blood in the last few seconds of life. I hang onto him, even as it slips beneath my collar, soaking my uniform.

'Let's get him out of here,' Bradford comes out of nowhere, reaching down in the dark, hot building. My mouth tastes like

sand, but I nod, feeling the life drain from my little brother. He's gone, but I'm not leaving him behind.

"Turner, you okay?" Bradford asks me, but his voice sounds funny. It sounds too light. "Turner?"

"*Turner.*" A soft touch lands on the back of my neck. "Are you okay?"

I shake my head as the noise fades, my iron grip around Gunner loosening. My heart drums in my ears as I look up, realizing suddenly I'm in the barn with the Christmas tree stand, my dog, and the woman I'm holding captive.

And I feel absolutely gutted.

If my brother could see the stupidity, the pain, the death, he'd be so fucking disappointed in me.

"Turner, will you please say something?" Em chokes out, clearly having read the situation for exactly what it was. "We don't have to put up the Christmas tree. I'm so sorry." Her voice cracks, and I blink, my heart slowing.

"No." I rub my eyes. "Just let me get it ready." I let go of Gunner and stand to my feet, keeping my back to her. I force myself to go through the motions, cutting it a second time, and drilling the holes while Em watches from afar, worry on her face.

The little flashback she saw was nothing, and I swallow hard as I consider what might happen. It always starts with the little flashbacks...

Which means I'm losing my grip on reality.

I eye Em as I slip past her with the tree and stand, Gunner staying close to me. He can feel my sanity slipping, too. The sense of impending doom is already heavy on my mind. I was worried about killing her and now, those worries are closing in. Now, I may just wake up and she be gone.

Like Thomas.

I focus only on my footsteps, counting them as I walk to the house. Maybe I've been deceiving myself since she showed up. I have a sick feeling of how this is all going to end for me. But still, Em has awakened the part of me that I thought died with Thomas...

The human side of me—the side of me that abhors everything I've become. The side that wanted a picket fence, a pretty wife, and yard full of kids. I'll never have it, and I know that. I don't deserve it, anyway. I glance back at Em, trudging behind me in silence, worry written all over her face.

I'm so fucking sorry, Em.

CHAPTER 18

EMERSYN

I DON'T KNOW that much about PTSD, but I heard the panic in Turner's voice as he shouted for Gunner. The response from Gunner nearly moved me to tears as he sprinted to the barn, like he was suddenly on a mission— with more urgency than he trailed me in the woods. He *knew* Turner needed him.

Now, even as I string popcorn on fishing line Turner gave me, working with what little I have to decorate, I can't shake the strange shift in Turner. He's got a strange, distant look in his eyes, and it's more unnerving than anything I've faced thus far.

Especially as he sits on the couch, still in his parka.

"Are you hungry?" I ask him as I finish my string of popcorn and stand to my feet.

"No," he answers me flatly, his eyes focused on the fire.

"Okay," I say quietly, threading the pitiful decoration around the Christmas tree he set by the door for me. I'm regretting everything about having him get it for me. I know it triggered whatever happened this afternoon, and I feel awful for it. At least hot and cold Turner looked less dead inside than this version—even him up in the room was less terrifying than *this* version.

When I finish, I approach him cautiously. "Aren't you hot in that?" I gesture to his coat.

He shakes his head, and stands to his feet, towering over me. "I'm going to bed."

"It's only seven o'clock," I reason, following him into the kitchen. He reaches to the cabinet above the fridge, pulling down a new bottle of prescription sleeping pills. I purse my lips as he heads down the hallway, noting his hands shaking.

"Turner, wait," I call after him, jogging to catch up as Gunner follows. I can't let him go up there alone, and I have a feeling he might not come back down. "Please." I grab his hand, tugging hard at him when he doesn't stop.

"Let me go. I just want to sleep for a while."

"Don't go," my voice wavers, and he finally turns back around to face me, his eyes no longer hardened like always. I see raw, gut-wrenching pain in them, and every fucking doubt I've ever had about him slips away.

"I'm a *very* bad person, Em," he rasps. "I've done things that no one ever should."

"It's okay," I tell him, reaching for his coat. I unzip it, pushing it off his shoulders. "I don't care what you've done."

"You should," he counters as I tug it the rest of the way off, forcing the bottle of pills out of his hand. They clatter to the floor, disappearing under the fabric of his parka. "What're you doing?"

"You're sweating," I breathe out, lifting the hem of his shirt.

"I'll be fine," he argues, but his voice is husky now.

I stand on my tiptoes, and he lets me pull it the rest of the way off. I take in his hard chest, brushing my fingertips over his skin, dipping to the snap on his snow pants. I undo it, feeling his erection beneath his sweatpants.

"Em," he groans. "You don't..." His voice trails off as I kneel, freeing him and brushing my lips against its tip. He sucks in a sharp breath, as I run my tongue around it, catching the precum. I take his cock into my mouth, the fullness sending a jolt of arousal through my body. "Stop," he says, nearly at a whisper. "Stop."

I do as he asks, ignoring the pang of rejection in my chest. "I just wanted to make you feel better."

He grabs my elbow and lifts me to my feet. "I know." His eyes are painfully soft as he kicks the rest of his pants off. "But let's do it right. If anyone's getting on their knees, it's me." Turner leans down and take my mouth possessively, his hand wrapping around my neck.

We stumble backward, my back hitting the wall. He strips off my sweatshirt and unhooks my bra, letting my breasts drop free. He palms them as he kisses his way down my jaw, and I hurriedly undo my jeans, shoving them and my underwear down my hips.

"So fucking eager," he breathes into my neck. "I don't understand you, Em."

"Likewise," I say, kicking off the rest of my clothes, his erection now pressing against my bare skin. "But I'll learn you, if you learn me."

"I'm unstable, Em." He kisses down my neck, stopping at my collarbone. "And I can't teach you something I don't know. No one has survived me." His words hit like a sledge-hammer to my heart, but his mouth finds my nipple then, sucking it into his mouth with force.

I thread my fingers in his dark hair, tipping my head back as his hand palms my other breast and he flits his tongue across my nipple. "I'll figure it out," I pant. "I'll figure you out."

He kneels, kissing his way down my stomach, pausing to look up at me. "I hope you do, angel. I really hope you do." Turner lifts me, catching me by surprise as my legs land on his shoulders and his arms wrap around my thighs.

My chest heaves as he buries his face between my legs, groaning as his tongue connects with me. "Oh fuck," I pant, as he circles my clit, pulling at me. I squirm against him, but he's relentless, sucking and licking, drawing me closer and closer to an orgasm.

"*Turner*," I cry as I near the edge. "I..." My voice trails off as I come, my thighs tightening around his head. He holds onto me, letting me grind against his face, drawing out as much pleasure as possible. My cries turn to sighs as he drops my legs, and then sweeps me up, carrying me into the bedroom.

His mouth crashes into mine as we collapse to the bed. He gives me no warning as he pushes himself into me, grunting with satisfaction. "You're so good, Em." He thrusts into me, biting down on my lips as he picks up his force.

I wrap my arms around his neck as we mesh skin with skin, baring more than just our bodies. All I can feel is him—his heat, his scent, his sanity slipping, if he ever had it from the beginning. As he comes inside of me, a guttural growl fills the room, laced with pain and pleasure.

"Oh fuck, Em," he groans into me, gripping me. "Why are you so sweet? Why aren't you trying to run away from me?" He buries his face in my hair, and I'm not sure who is holding who in the moment.

"Do you still have to go upstairs now?" I whisper when he finally releases me, propping himself up on his elbows.

He searches my eyes, his fingers brushing across my cheek. "I can stay here with you. Just let me shower."

I nod, resting my hand over his. "Okay."

He slides off me and then the bed, heading for the bathroom. I take in the shadow of him, noting that he leaves the door open as he slips into the shower. I watch him through the glass, wondering what he's thinking, and if he's even close to being okay.

And is it selfish of me to think that I could be enough for him? Could I give him something to keep his mind here? I mean, his brother left him. What if I didn't? What if I chose to stay? Could he love me?

The questions swim around my head as I lay there, watching Turner's shadow in the shower. *I'm fucking crazy for falling for him. He killed Adam. God knows who else he's killed. He's threatened to kill me, too.*

But for some reason, I really don't think he will.

Turner steps out of the shower then, toweling off and heading in my direction. He stops a couple feet from the door. "Were you just staring at me the whole time?"

I blush. "Whoops. Sorry."

He grins at me, letting out a chuckle. "It's fine. It's just been a long time since anyone has tried to catch a glimpse of me naked."

"I bet that's weird for you," I say, following him as he climbs into bed beside me, tugging the covers up around both of us.

"Yeah, I guess so." He pulls me into his chest, and I wrap my arm around him, snuggling into his chest again. "So you read the letters on the desk?"

"Yeah," I say, feeling him tense beneath me. "I also read your brother's journal." He stops breathing at the mention of that, and I suddenly regret mentioning. "I'm sorry. I shouldn't have. I was just... I just wanted to know who you are. I don't know. It was absolutely heartbreaking—what you went through," I feel myself rambling, terrified of the reaction that he's going to have, desperate to stave off his explosion. I don't have clothes on to go sprinting into the night. "Turner, I'm so sorry."

He audibly swallows. "I haven't read his journal. I, uh, couldn't stomach that."

"There's not a lot in there," I say quietly. "I... Um... I'm sorry that he left you when you were really going through it."

"What?" Turner's reaction takes me by surprise.

"That he left?" I offer it out there again.

"Mm," is all he says, then kissing the top of my head. He falls into silence after that, but in ten or so minutes of me holding my breath, he falls asleep, his breaths deep and even. I lay against him, listening to him like that, until I finally catch myself drifting off into a haze of slumber as well. However, I still can't shake that I'm missing a piece of his complicated puzzle...

And it leaves me with a bad, *bad* feeling in my gut.

CHAPTER 19

TURNER

I DON'T FALL ASLEEP HOLDING Emersyn. I just let her think I do. I can't stop wondering about the journal upstairs. I didn't go through his things after everything happened. I knew that my psyche couldn't handle it, but...

She thinks he actually left.

She has no idea he's buried in my backyard.

Swallowing hard, I unentangle myself from her, slipping out of the bed in total silence. I glance at the window. It's almost sunup. I need to finish Em's present, which is a second reason I have to brave Tommy's room. I need a chain —and the only one I have is from my dog tags, which are in the box at the top of the closet upstairs. I only know that, because I saw it once, back when I was trying to cope instead of just descend into darkness.

I pad out of the room, carefully shutting the door. If something goes terribly wrong, she'll be hopefully out of sight and out of mind—*maybe*. I stop at the pile of clothes in the hallway, and fish out the wooden pendent I made for her.

I then start the ascent to the second floor. I've done it hundreds of times since everything happened, but this time, it feels like I might be taking a walk to my doom. *Maybe I should just leave the journal. I'll just get the chain.*

My new plan brings me little relief as I turn the knob and creep inside the room. I shut the door behind me, and kick on the light. "Just get the chain," I tell myself. "Just the chain." I make my way across the floors, ignoring the pictures, obituaries, and everything else.

My hands are trembling by the time I make it to the closet door, but it doesn't cloud my mind. I take a deep breath, and open the door, ignoring Thomas's things— which are still there, covered in a thick layer of dust. I should've done something with it all, but I couldn't bring myself to. If Em would've opened the closet, maybe then she would've realized that Thomas is a different kind of gone.

I abandoned him, not the other way around.

Swallowing the knot in my throat, I reach up and grab the cardboard box, tucked in the back right corner. I pull it down, and set it on the floor, staring at the words scrawled in black sharpie marker.

Turner's Keepsakes.

I pop my jaw, as I kneel beside it, carefully peeling back the tape—tape that Tommy put there. He was the one who collected all my shit, put it all together, and then made sure it didn't get lost in transit. He did everything for me, and I killed him. I leave the tape hanging off the side and fold back the lid.

"For fuck's sake," I mutter, pinching the bridge of my nose as I flip it open. There on top is a folder, and I pull it out, dropping it on the floorboard beside me. It's more than likely discharge information and whatever else they felt the need to send me home with. I lean over the box and start sifting through the contents, trying not to look too hard at the patches and pictures.

I used to love this life. The thought comes without warning, leaving a sick taste in my mouth. That was a long time ago, and I don't know how I could say I loved it when it took my brother and my sanity. *But did it take my sanity? Or was I always destined to fuck up like this?*

Pushing it away, I finally locate the dog tags at the bottom. I don't look at them. I unclip the chain and slide it out, dropping the tags back into the box. Taking a deep breath, I take out the pendent and slide it through. I nearly scoff at how childish it looks. The woman is probably used to diamonds and gold, not fucking cedar and cheap silver.

I stand to my feet, surprised I'm not losing it, and walk over to Tommy's desk, opening the top drawer and pulling out a blank piece of card stock. I grab a pen, and click it, hovering over the paper. *What the hell do I say?* I stare at it for a few moments longer, and then scribble something down, signing my name at the bottom.

Only then, when I'm all finished and the pendent with its chain is laying on the desk, do I start to think about the journal again. I open each drawer, and it takes until I make it to the bottom before I find the leather-bound book. My heart thrums in my ears as I pick it up, knowing I shouldn't.

Don't fucking do it.

But the warning to myself is useless. I flip the damn journal open, and it falls to the last entry on the day before Thomas died, and as I read his final words.

December 24, 2013...

I snap the book shut and toss it into the drawer, slamming it shut. "Permanently broken," I say the words aloud. "You thought I was permanently broken." I stare at the now-closed drawer, my ears beginning to ring, but it's not the war that comes rushing back this time. It's Christmas.

"I don't know why you don't want to put up a Christmas tree," Thomas scoffs as he pours milk into his bowl of cereal. His hair is already graying, and I'm pretty sure it's because of me. He's three inches taller than me, and with little effort, he could've outdone me at my best. He looks up at me. "I've done it for years here, and never once caught the cabin on fire."

I stare at him, my heart pounding in my ears. "I don't know. Just seems like a bad idea." I don't really care about the Christmas tree. I just don't want to think about the memories that go with it. My head has been buzzing the last few days, my body's felt antsy, and I can't figure out what's going on. Maybe I just need to get out of the house for a while.

"Hey," Tommy calls after me as I head outside, Gunner hopping down from the couch to follow me. "Where are you going?"

"A walk," I call over my shoulder to him as I step out into the frigid December air. It's been mild this winter, but the chill

has finally settled in. I rub my hands together, as my boots crunch in the snow.

"You need a coat," Thomas appears in the threshold of the backdoor. "What's going on with you? I noticed Gunner keeps—"

"He doesn't know what he's doing. I'm fine," I cut him off. "He needs more training or something."

"Are you... Are you sure?" Tommy joins, falling in step beside me. "Something is off, Turner. You can talk to me about what's going on. I can take you to see Dr. Newcomb next week. We can work this out. Maybe you should trying an in-house treatment?"

I turn to face him, throwing my hands up. "Why do you always assume something is fucking wrong with me? Maybe if you quit assuming that, I wouldn't feel so... Messed up."

"You've got that distant, dead look in your eyes." His expression is riddled with concern, and I hate it. I hate his sympathy. I hate the torture and isolation I've brought on him. He reaches out and touches my shoulder.

My head explodes, the touch searing through my body like a fire. Gunner barks at me. Tommy removes his hand and backs away...

And then it all goes dark.

I wake up in the snow, my body sore and my head hurting. I peer down at my hands, covered in dried blood. Gunner whines beside me, and I turn to him, panic thrumming through my body.

"What did I do?" I ask him, my voice shaking. "What did I do?"

But the limp body a few feet away, laying in the snow tells me everything. I immediately crawl to him, my knee smashing into something hard. I glance down to see my rifle. Why is he out here? Why do I have my rifle? *Panic and dread flush through my system as I crawl to my brother.*

"Tommy?" I choke out. "Tommy." I grab his arm and roll him over. His face is contorted with pain. His hands grip his chest.

"It's okay," he whispers.

I shake my head, tears blurring my vision. "What did I do? What happened?"

Blood slips from his lips, rolling down his chin. "You snapped."

"But I don't remember," I say quickly. "I don't remember it. I gotta call... I need to call an ambulance, Tommy." I go for his cell phone in his jacket, my hands shaking as I try to unlock it, my numb hands not working right.

Tommy's hand stops me, knocking the phone out of my hand. "Don't."

"Why?" I exasperate, trying to fish it out of the snow.

He lets out a pained breath, and I recognize it. It's death, bearing down on him. "You don't belong in prison for this."

"I don't want to hurt people," I plead with him. "If I'm there I won't..."

His head shakes. "You just have to figure out..." Blood spurts from his mouth again and I try to wipe it away. "You have to figure out how to stop it, feed the monster, something."

"What?" I exasperate, panic, guilt, and dread suffocating me. "Do I just stay here by myself? What am I supposed to do?"

"Bury me under my favorite tree." His eyes close, and then he tremors with death, his breaths ceasing. I shake him violently, but it's too late.

I just fucking killed my brother.

I suck in a gulp of air as a hot breath pants on my face. I come to, staring into the face of Gunner, his wet nose nudging me. I stare into his chocolate-brown eyes, hating everything about myself in the moment. Rage toward myself sears through my body. It's a flood of heat, coursing through my veins like a drug—but the realization is still there, even in my descent into madness.

All the killing I did to try and feed the monster after Thomas's death, I tried to say was in the name of trespassing, but it was just an attempt to stave off the pain. And it's time for it to end. I rise to my feet, and with numb, methodical movements, I exit the room.

My footsteps are quiet on the stairs as I make my way out into the snow. There's only one thing that Em really needs for Christmas. There's only one thing I really want to do for her—and that's to fucking save her from me.

And that's exactly what I'm going to do.

CHAPTER 20

EMERSYN

THE DOOR SLAMMING jars me from my sleep, and I startle awake, my eyes drifting up to the clock. It's almost nine o'clock in the morning. As the time registers in my mind, the door to the bedroom creaks open, and Turner's figure appears in the doorway.

"Morning," I greet him, my voice groggy with sleep.

He doesn't say anything as he takes a step toward me and slams the door shut behind him. My heart jumps to my throat as I meet his dark gaze, full of emotion and hatred.

"Are you—"

"Shut up, Em," he growls, ripping his shirt over his head. "Just shut up." He strips down within seconds, coming for me. I find myself bracing as he rips the covers off, exposing me in just an oversized T-shirt.

"Turner," I whimper as he grabs my ankles and drags me toward him. He wastes no time as he plunges into me, and I let out a cry with the force behind his movements. "Slow down," I cry out as he pounds into me, his iron grip painful around my waist. "*Turner*," tears well up in my eyes as I try to push against him.

He finally lifts his gaze from where we're joined to meet my eyes, and he lets out a heavy breath. "You're an angel, Em, and I'm so fucking sorry you landed in hell."

My lip trembles as I push myself upward, grabbing his jaw and forcing his lips to mine. He's hesitant at first, but then attacks my mouth, devouring me with a coercive kiss. I taste his anger, pain, and something else, as he returns to thrusting into me. His hips slam against mine, and I moan into Turner's mouth as he lifts me from the bed. He uses me like a ragdoll, his strong arms jarring my hips back and forth.

I fall into motion with him, grinding against his body and catching my own high. Pleasure begins to build as his movements shift from forceful to passionate, his growls morphing to groans.

"Oh shit, Em," he rasps, breaking our kiss and holding my gaze. "You're everything. You're fucking everything."

I orgasm at his words, a wave of intense pleasure rolling over my body as my pussy clenches around him. I cry out his name, and his eyes close, his face growing peaceful. My fingers latch around his head, and I pull his mouth to mine again. He pumps into me, his kisses slowing as he moans, exploding inside of me.

He rests his forehead against mine. "Thank you for saving me, Em."

I catch my breath, my heart jumping to my throat. "Turner..."

He shakes his head. "You're special, Em, and for whatever reason you ended up here, I'll spend eternity thankful for it." With that, he rolls off me abruptly, slides off the bed, and starts to get dressed again.

I watch him, slowly climbing out of bed myself. I desperately need a shower, and as I make my way to the bathroom, Turner reaches for me, threading his arm around my waist. I peer up at him, and the somber expression on his face sends a wave of panic through my body.

"What's wrong, Turner?"

"Nothing at all," he smiles, leaning down to press a kiss to my lips. It's charged with emotion, and I allow myself to linger it in for a few moments. As he pulls away, he kisses my forehead. "Merry Christmas, Em."

"It's Christmas Eve," I say carefully.

"Might as well be Christmas, angel." He brushes his fingertips along my jaw and then disappears from the room, heading upstairs. I step into the bathroom, a strange feeling hanging over my body as I turn on the water. Something is wrong... Or maybe I'm just being paranoid?

I spend the next forty-five minutes, standing under the hot water until it runs cold. My mind replays the entirety of my time at the cabin, and I wonder what life is like outside of the cabin—what my family is thinking right now. Are they worried? Are they pushing for people to look for me? I mean, I know Adam would've told them, right?

A sigh escapes my lips, and I find myself unmoved by the thoughts, more consumed by the silence in the house. I dress in a pair of fleece leggings and red sweater, leaving my damp

ANNIE WILD

hair down. When I step out of the bedroom, I find Gunner, sitting by the backdoor.

"Turner," I call out. "I think Gunner needs to go to the bathroom." I glance around the cabin, not seeing any signs of him. Turner wouldn't go outside without Gunner, and so I figure he's upstairs, which brings along some sort of alarm in my head. I start to think about the pills, and I head back to down the hallway, spotting the folded clothes on the first step of the stairwell.

Ours from last night. I step over them, noting the still-full pill bottle sitting beside my shirt. I head upstairs, my heart rate picking up as I reach the top. The door to the spare room is...*open.* A cold draft rushes around me, and I brace myself for what I'll find, but when I step inside, I only see an open box in the middle of the floor.

I furrow my brow as I walk over to it, seeing *Turner's Keepsakes* scrawled on the side. Half the contents are spilled on the floor, and as much as I want to sit and go through them, the sight triggers an urge to find Turner instead. I spin on my heels, but not before catching sight of the open drawer at the desk.

Rushing over to it, I don't see anything missing, but I *do* see a beautifully hand carved wooden heart on a chain. I pick it up, seeing the intricate flowers carved, and an *E* right in the center. I roll it over in my palm, emotions welling up in my chest. My eyes then drop to the small, folded cardstock. I unfold it, reading the note.

Merry Christmas,

Em. I hope you find this. You reminded me of the person I

once was—and wish I could still be. You saved me, and now, I have to save you from me.

Love,

Turner

I shove the note in my pocket and grip the locket in my hand as panic washes over my entire body. My mind takes me back to the peaceful expression on Turner's face, and I sprint from the room, thundering down the stairs. Gunner breaks into a bark at the door, as I shove my feet into my shoes. I stop to fasten the chain around my neck, and then grab my jacket, tearing through the open door.

"Find him," I scream to Gunner. "Find him," I repeat, my voice breaking. I scan the area, and that's when I spot a single wooden cross, uncovered by the winds blowing from the east instead of north. As I tug on my coat, I run toward it, my stomach sinking as I come close enough to read the name etched on it.

Thomas Robert Martin

05/17/1980 – 12/25/2013

A sob tears from my chest. Thomas *never* left, and I don't have to ask to know the answer to this question. Tears slip down my cheeks, as I spin around, searching for Gunner. He scratches at the barn walk-through door, and I rush for it, turning the knob.

It's locked.

I stop, trying to listen over my pounding heart. I hear *something* on the other side. I jiggle the doorknob again. "Turner," I shout, banging my fist on the door. "Turner, let me in."

Nothing.

"Turner," I scream at the top of my lungs, slamming my fists so hard they begin to ache. "*Please.*" Tears roll down my cheeks freely, as Gunner bays from behind me, his panic reflecting mine. I don't know how to break in. I barrel my shoulder into the door as hard as I can, begging and pleading for the old frame to give way to my weight.

Adrenaline surges through my body as I slam against the door once more, and the wood splits—but it doesn't give. I yell his name again, begging him to let me inside. Gunner's panicked barks drown out the sound of anything else as he begins to jump and scratch at the door. I feel as though I'm losing touch as I kick with all my strength, my breaths heavy and desperate for oxygen. I throw my body at it one more fucking time.

And it splinters, giving way and finally letting me inside.

I fall into the darkness, landing on my shoulder. I swallow the staggering pain and scramble to my feet, searching for Turner. Gunner darts past me, heading to the back of the barn, his feet silently moving across the concrete floors. I sprint after him, not even bothered by the sight of Adam's jeep. I don't care.

I *really* don't care.

My footsteps echo as I make it to the dimly lit area, reaching stacks of boxes and tubs, labeled with different things—all of it Turner's. As I scan around myself, squinting in the dark, I meet his gaze.

And the barrel of a gun.

"Get out of here, Em," he says, his voice monotone. "I

unburied your truck. The roads were cleared last night. Take Gunner. Don't make me force you."

I step toward him, where he's sitting in an old, dusty chair. "Don't do this, Turner."

He shakes his head at me, cocking the hammer. "You think you know me, but you don't have the slightest idea of what I've done."

"You killed your brother," I throw out the assumption. "And my guess is Adam doesn't make number two."

His eyes alight with irritation. "No. He's number nine. Seven other people trespassed on this place, and I did what I did."

I nod, surprisingly less terrified than I expected myself to be. I take another step, and his hand trembles, his finger on the trigger. "If you shoot me, you'll regret it."

"You're right," he says flatly. "But moments later, I'll be burning in hell, anyway."

"Don't leave Gunner alone," I reason, my voice softening at the pain in his eyes. "We can fix this... You're not too far gone, Turner."

"Yes, I am," he snaps, his eyes boring into mine. "Tommy told me before he went cold to find a way to appease the monster in me—and I found my way, killing people who came here when they shouldn't—and now, I don't think that's what he meant. But it's too late to change it."

"Cycles can be broken," I reason, inching closer as Gunner backs away, sitting. I reach out, and in one swift move, I take the gun from his hand. He doesn't fight me for it, nor does he stop me from straddling him, taking a seat in his lap.

"What're you doing, Em?" he groans. "I'm finally going to do what needs to be done, and you're forcing me to get violent."

I press the barrel to his temple, my heart throbbing in my head. "Tell me everything. I want to hear it all."

He meets my gaze. "I'd rather you just pull the trigger."

CHAPTER 21

TURNER

THERE'S anger in her eyes. I know she thinks I'm weak, but that's not true. If I was weak, I'd give in to the urge I had to kill her, and bury her body next to my brother's. I'm finally strong enough, because of her, to do what should've been done a long time ago. Sometimes, it's better to put a wounded animal out of its misery than let it live with its disability.

"I'll pull the trigger," Em says, her voice calm and collected. "And then I'll take Gunner and I'll leave this hell I was trapped in for weeks. Don't you worry."

My chest swells. "Good girl."

A tear rolls down her cheek as her lower lip trembles. "But first, I want you to tell me *everything*." Her voice strains as she presses it harder into my temple, doing the job I planned to do myself—and *will* do myself. I won't let her be the one who pulls the trigger.

But I'll let her feel in control in this moment.

"Where do you want me to start?" I ask her, a strange calmness settling in my body.

"What happened to your brother?"

I let out a long, heavy sigh. "I killed him."

"How?" she demands, her eyes alight with *anger*. "How did you kill him?"

"I shot him with my rifle. Something was wrong with me," I begin, the truth spilling easier than I expected. "I got this weird urge, like I was in the middle of war—but there weren't any flashbacks. It all just went dark."

She nods. "He could tell something was wrong, but Gunner helps you, yeah?"

I smile up at her, my eyes growing wet. "He's a damn good dog, and the only reason I'm still here—but that was before you showed up. You can take him and give him a good life."

"He'd be lost without you."

"He'd be less stressed," I chuckle, wiping away the first tear I've cried in decades.

Em's lip quivers, but she holds it together. "Keep going. What happened?"

I blow out a breath. "I...I went outside. He went with me —Gunner, too. I just needed air. Or something?" I pause, shaking my head. "I felt off. I didn't have a gun with me at the time. He said something to me? He told me I needed to get help and he would take me to see my doctor. I argued with him, saying nothing was wrong, but then he said I had this *dead, distant* look in my eyes. I'd seen it myself. It scared me, Em."

"Then what?"

"Then it all went dark. I don't know what happened." I can't look her in the face as I finish, explaining the gun, my dying brother, and the way I buried him where he asked. "I wanted to call the cops, and turn myself in. I knew I'd be committed. That's what they wanted to do when I had my first...*episode.*"

She nods. "At the grocery store."

My eyes widen with surprise. "How do you know?"

"The journal. Your parents got in a car accident on the way to pick you up, and your brother went to them instead of you."

"He did the right thing," I say, ignoring the blast of grief in my chest. "I guess technically I've killed three of my four dead family members." I bite down on the inside of my cheek.

"No," she reasons, shaking her head as she sinks deeper into my lap, her body warm against mine. "No, you didn't. That's not how it works. If a kid is waiting for their mom to pick them up from school, and she dies on the way there, it's not the kid's fault."

"Kid's probably not playing war in the bathroom, either."

"Still doesn't make it your fault."

"Okay, but the others are."

Emersyn nods. "Yeah, they are. Why don't you tell me what you did?"

Unable to meet her eyes, I explain the first time I caught a hunter trespassing, he tried to shoot, but I was faster—and then every time someone else was caught, I shot first and never asked questions. I buried them all, too, but didn't put crosses in the ground.

"Very interesting," she remarks, confusion filling her face. "Though, I suppose one could argue they were in the wrong for trespassing."

"Maybe. It wasn't until you, that I..." My voice trails off as I gather my wits. "That I felt something again. Now, you know what I am."

"And what are you, really?" her question comes out in a whisper as the fingers of her free hand trace my cheek, grazing the trail of moisture.

"A psychopath," I answer her, feeling myself harden. "That's what I am."

Emersyn falls into silence, sniffling as fresh tears slip down her cheeks. I take in the sight of her, her still-damp hair spilling over her shoulders, her eyes red from the tears, and my chain around her neck. She stiffens as I reach up and tug the small heart out from under her sweater.

"Guess you found it." I run my finger over the *E.* "Kind of elementary."

Her hand comes to mine, brushing over it softly, while the barrel still digs into my temple. Maybe she *is* in control, because I have never wanted to be a good man so badly—and I'd do absolutely anything the woman told me to.

"It's the best Christmas gift I've gotten in years," she says, holding my gaze. "I think it's beautiful."

"I always wanted to find a girl to wear my chain," another piece of my past spills from my lips. "It's that stupid?" I look up at her. "I wanted the whole thing—the white picket fence, the wife, and the kids. Can you imagine me, a fucking nutcase, with kids? Guaranteed that they'd end up troubled and fucked in the head."

She smiles, squeezing my hand. "What a beautiful life you could have had."

"Yeah, I know," I laugh. "Isn't that crazy? I thought I was a hero once, Em. I thought I was Superman, coming to save the day every time I went on a mission. By the time I made it home, I was already turning into a villain—and then I realized I've always been the villain in someone else's story. I couldn't find peace unless I was causing violence."

She nods in understanding, and my body relaxes underneath her. It's like a therapy session, only with a beautiful, compassionate woman sitting on my lap. Never mind the gun to my head. We fall into silence, and I wait, wait for her to say something else. But she doesn't.

It must be time. She's heard enough.

I turn my head to Gunner, sitting there, no longer panting with panic or worry. He no longer appears concerned, and for some reason that brings a deeper sense of peace in addition to the rest. It's *finally* over. No more nights with pills. No more spilling blood. No more pain.

I turn my head back to Em, who's got a whole river of tears rolling down her cheeks. "You don't have to do it, baby," my voice sounds so gentle, so sweet, reaching a level of empathy I haven't felt in years.

"Final words," she demands.

I shake my head. "I'd never give you that burden. Just

know that *if* I somehow avoid going to hell, I'll keep an eye on you, Em—and if I get that kind of grace, I'll see you on the other side." My hand lands on hers, my index finger sliding over the trigger. "Let me do it. Close your eyes."

She swallows audibly, Gunner lets out a pained bay, echoing in the emptiness of silence.

And then *she* pulls the trigger.

CHAPTER 22

EMERSYN

I KNOW WHAT I DID. But he deserved it.

As his eyes flicker open at the gunshot right behind his head, I throw the weapon to the floor, metal skidding against concrete the only sound between us.

His eyes narrow. "You missed."

"No, I didn't," I answer him. "I did exactly what I should have. You're not dying." I fist his collar with newfound anger, and then lean down, brushing my nose to his. "You're getting fucking *help.*"

"The hell I am," He growls back at me. "I want *peace,* Emersyn."

I shake my head, swinging my leg off him and standing to my feet. "Then you'll have to kill me, Turner, but even then, I'll fucking haunt you."

Turner glares at me. "I thought you understood me, but *clearly* you don't." He rises, towering over me. "You think that I'll just magically be fixed, huh?" His hand shoots out, wrapping around my arm and dragging me toward him.

I wrap my hands around his, trying to pry his fingers from around me. "I *don't* think that. I just want you to stay—"

"You're fucking *selfish*," he roars at me, dropping his hand. Turner spins around and in one swift kick sends the chair flying across the barn as I stumble and fall hard onto the concrete. I swallow the pain shooting up my spine as I watch him sweep up the pistol from the floor, pointing it at me.

"Go ahead," I snap at him as he stalks toward me. "Kill me, and *then* you can reevaluate who's the fucking selfish one in the room, but you know," I pause, ignoring the fear thrumming through my body. "Your brother didn't want you to die. He didn't turn you in, because he believed you could get better."

"Yeah, jokes on him," he scoffs. "I'm too far gone."

Defeat riddles my chest, and my shoulders drop. "Nothing I can say is going to change your mind, so go ahead." I gaze down at my hands, trembling as I wrap them around me, mentally readying myself for my end. "Just make sure you find a way to let my fucking family know. I have people who will miss me."

Turner says nothing in response, looming over me like the Grim Reaper, the gun still hovering near my head. I squeeze my eyes shut. Unlike me, I know Turner will make good on his threat. I never could've killed him. I don't kill the people I love like he does. And while the realization of having feelings for him is shocking, it's not nearly as shocking as the way I'm *okay* with those feelings.

"It was always going to end like this," I say under my breath, thinking back through it all..

"What?" Turner demands, his voice thick. "What did you say?"

I tip my head back, meeting his red-eyed gaze with my own equally heartbroken one. "It was always going to end like this. You said it from the very beginning. There was never going to be an alternate ending like I let myself believe. Even till the very end, when I knew it all, I believed you could change, and I think that's the biggest mistake I made here." My chest tightens with pain, and I choke back a fresh sob.

Turner drops to his knees in front of me, resting against his heels. He ejects the magazine and then the bullet from the chamber. "Better?" He tosses it across the floor again. "I don't have it in me, Em. I can't kill you when I'm still *here*. I'd only ever hurt you if... If I'm *not*—and that's what scares me."

I reach for him, wrapping my arms around his neck. He kisses my cheek, threading his arm around my waist. His lips graze across my skin, and as I'm pressed against him, I can feel his heartbeat, alive and well—even if his mind isn't.

Maybe I am being selfish. I suck in a sharp breath as I lean away, studying his face. "I'm sorry. I want what's best for you."

"Em," he says, his voice soft as he thumbs away the tears from my cheeks. "We can figure it out, but this..." Turner's gaze jumps to the gun on the floor. "This isn't the way to do it. I'm too tired of spilling blood, and while I think I belong in the ground, you don't—and I'll respect that."

"That's the only reason?"

He chuckles, a ghost of a smile appearing on his face. "I mean, right now, that's what I've got."

I mirror it batting away fresh tears. "I'm sorry I didn't get you anything for Christmas. I don't have skills like this." I brush my finger over the necklace. "It's incredible."

"This was by far, the best Christmas I've had in years." He runs his hand along my outer thigh. "You gave me more than you realize." I nod, throwing myself into him again and holding on tight. "I'll be good," Turner murmurs into my hair. "I can be good for you. It'll just take me some time to figure it out."

"I know," I say, clinging to him. I was just minutes away from losing him forever, and the reality of that sinks in with every passing moment. "It'll be okay. We'll figure it out."

Turner kisses the top of my head, and then lifts me up, wrapping his arms around my ass. "I'm tired of being in here."

He carries me out, breathing in deeply as we reach the fresh air. "I had no idea you had it in you to kick in a door."

I laugh. "Me either, but desperate times call for desperate measures, I guess."

Shaking his head, he steps up onto the back porch, and then heads inside of the cabin. He shuts the door behind Gunner, and then heads straight for the bedroom. He shuts the dog out, and then drops me down on the bed.

He climbs onto it beside me, and then cups my cheek in

his hand. "You're the best unplanned gift I've ever gotten." Turner leans down and presses his lips to mine, and I nip at his lower lip. Groaning, he glides his hand to the bottom of my sweater, tugging it up over my head.

I unsnap my bra and then kick off my shoes as he tugs at my leggings. I then go for his shirt, pulling it off him. We finish methodically undressing each other, and I soak it in. I have no freaking idea what we're going to do when this holiday is over—when real life comes back.

When everyone finds out that Adam is gone. It's going to be a whirlwind of scrutiny and coverups, but if it makes me a bad person to already know I'll cover for him, then so be it. He uses his knee to part my legs, situating himself between them.

I nip at his bottom lip, drawing out a groan from deep in his chest. "I don't care if you're dangerous. I still want you."

"You're a brave woman," he counters, grabbing my chin and running his thumb along my mouth. He presses against my lips, and I suck it into the warmth of my mouth. Turner watches me with a dark expression, tinged with lust and desire. The tip of his cock brushes my entrance, and I rock my hips toward him, desperate to have him again.

I don't care if he's fucking insane.

I'm pretty sure I am, too.

"Fuck, Em," he rasps as he presses himself into my pussy, already soaked and ready for him. "You always feel so good." His breaths deepen as he fills me the rest of the way, his hooded eyes hazy as they hold mine.

He pulls his thumb from my mouth, and I drop back on

the bed, gazing up at him. His features are softer as he thrusts in and out of me, dropping his head to kiss my lips. And even then, his kiss is more careful and slower, as if he's purposefully taking his time with me.

I thread my fingers through his dark locks, as his mouth trails down my jaw, neck, and then dips lower to my chest. I grind against him, riding the high as arousal pumps through my body, drawing me toward the edge. My nails dig into his scalp as I arch my back.

"*Turner*," I cry out his name as I crash around him, the walls of my pussy pulsing with pleasure as he sucks in my breast, circling my nipple with his tongue. I cling to him as he thrusts through my climax, drawing it out as he picks up his pace.

"I love it when you come," he pants into my chest, palming and kissing me with an added air of hunger now. He pumps into me over and over, and I watch him, the god of a man, losing his control inside of me.

It's almost spiritual, the way he moves and fucks me. He's not thinking about his past or future—and he's not fighting urges for violence. He's just himself, and as he explodes inside of me, filling me with his cum, he groans out my name.

"Emersyn," he rumbles, the deep tenor in his voice shaking the walls of my chest cavity. He locks eyes with me before he collapses, pulling out and resting his head against my upper abdomen.

I stroke his hair as we lay there, lost in the moment and

still disconnected from reality. "Turner," I say, running my fingers through his hair once more. "I don't want to leave."

His breaths slow but he doesn't look up at me. "Then don't."

"People will wonder where I am, and not to mention, there's also the issue of my ex-boyfriend..."

He stiffens at that, pushing himself up off the bed. "We don't have to make it complicated. You ended up here. He ended up God knows where, out searching for you—or whatever."

"And what about my phone?"

Turner's brow furrows. "What about it?"

"I don't have one anymore, and my guess is that people will want to know why." The thought starts to give me anxiety, bursting through the illusion that I could somehow stay quietly with Turner for the rest of my life.

"Hey," Turner tips my chin toward him. "It's all okay. I'll figure it out. It's easy to say you lost your phone in the blizzard."

"Adam's jeep is in your barn," I reason, as Turner shifts up the bed and wraps his arms around me. "What are we supposed to do about that?"

"I've gotten rid of vehicles before." His voice is quiet. "I'll put it in the river not far from here. I'll take care of that. You don't have to worry about it, Em. I've got it."

"You buried your brother under a tree that could easily be spotted if the cops came and searched your place." I turn to him, starting to feel a sense of worry. "What would happen?"

"I don't know." He shrugs. "Maybe I'd go to prison. Maybe that wouldn't be the end of the world. I don't care. I did what I did." The sincerity in his voice calms my mind, but only for a split second. Gunner lets out a bark, and Turner's entire expression grows stone cold.

"What is it?" I ask him as he lunges off the bed, grabbing his clothes.

Just as he opens his mouth to answer me, I hear it.

Sirens.

CHAPTER 23

TURNER

I knew this would happen eventually. I swallow the apprehension as I finish dressing and head for the front door of the cabin. I opened the gate this morning, thinking that Emersyn and Gunner would be leaving, and I'd be left to decompose in the barn. Instead, I'm now trudging out into the afternoon to face cops.

Merry Christmas to me.

"Thomas Martin?" the officer calls out as he climbs out of his SUV, parked behind Em's dug out truck.

"Turner," I correct him, coming down the steps to greet the officer. He's around my age, and honestly, is a rather puny guy with gray hair and mustache. I could take him, but that would be an even worse idea than letting myself live. "Thomas is my brother."

"Ah, right. I forgot you moved in all those years ago. Never really see much of you." He watches my reaction with icy blue eyes, already full of suspicion.

"Yeah, I don't get out much," I answer him flatly. "What can I do for you?"

He points to the truck. "For starters, you can tell me why this truck is in your driveway."

I shrug. "Yeah, it's Emersyn's. She accidentally pulled in here at the start of the blizzard. Got stuck. I dug her out this morning when the roads were finally cleared."

"And *where* is she?" He lightens a little, but not much. "She hasn't been in contact with any of her family. They've been worried."

"She's inside," I answer. "She lost her phone when she was walking up here. I don't have a phone, but I'm sure you know that."

"That's what I've heard," he grunts, just as the door of the cabin opens, and out walks Emersyn, dressed and wrapped up in her parka. I glance back at her, a slight smile on her face as she joins us.

"You must be Miss Lewis," the officer says to her.

"I am..." Her voice trails off, and if she's nervous, I can't tell. "My GPS sent me the wrong way and then I ended up here."

"I see that. Have you by chance spoken with Adam Shatz since your arrival here?" His eyes bore into hers, and my stomach knots up at the scrutiny.

She hesitates, like she's thinking. "Well, I mean, yes and no. I was on the phone with him when I pulled in the driveway. I thought it was their family cabin, but I think I got really turned around. I dropped my phone in the snow when I was trying to make it to the cabin from here." She pauses again, looking downtrodden. "I haven't spoken to him since. I was planning on trying to either find the cabin or maybe drive to town for a new cell phone today. I'm not a great driver in snow," she adds, her cheeks flushing.

Fuck, she is really playing this well.

He nods. "I see. Well, I hate to break it to you, ma'am, but your ex-boyfriend is missing, too. He apparently called family, stating that he was going to look for you when the snow stopped—and that the two of you had gotten into a fight, breaking up on the way. He stated you turned into the wrong driveway."

Her face falls, and she *actually* looks heartbroken, shocked, and taken aback. "Yeah, to my surprise, he wasn't so serious about us. I broke up with him, but I don't understand? How can he be missing?"

"Cameras at his place show that he left his residence as soon as the snow stopped from the first storm. He never returned. Though, I have to admit, I'm still trying to figure out how you ended up *here*. The Shatz cabin is nearly twelve miles to the east of here."

"Wait, what?" She shakes her head. "My GPS was taking me down this road."

He nods. "This address actually only differs by one road number, so it's not all that surprising you ended up way out here."

She nods. "I'm just lucky I ended up here instead of freezing to death." She doesn't look at me as she says the words, but they seem so ironic, given all the hell I've put her through—and now, she's so graceful and earnest with her answers.

Maybe I'm not the only psychopath in this relationship.

"Well, I'm glad I thought to head this way," the officer continues. "I need to radio this in. Your family will be relieved to find you in good health." As he goes to step away, Em reaches out, touching his shoulder.

"But please tell me search and rescue is looking for Adam, right? Like he can drive in this weather, but... But how long has he been missing? I don't—"

"Ma'am," he gives her a pained expression. "No matter how well someone is accustomed to this weather, blizzard conditions are dangerous. Best case scenario at this point, he's going to show up after digging himself out, but..." He lets out a sigh. "Yes, we have recovery teams out searching now."

"Recovery?" she echoes him, her voice breaking. "I thought you said he might show back up."

"Just trying to be hopeful," he says, giving Em a sympathetic expression. "It's a slim chance, but it's the best-case scenario at this point." The officer then eyes me. "I'm just glad I have some good news to report. Your family is already on a flight here."

Oh shit. Her family is coming? I can't handle that. My heart jumps to my throat, the bubble I was living in up until that point bursting. *I can't let her stay here with me. She has to go home. I'll never make the transition right now.*

Em continues to chat with the officer, bullshitting him with sociopathic lies about her time here, and her worries for

Adam. I stand outside in the cold, watching it unfold in surreal time with my arms folded across my chest. I *want* to be the guy for Em—but I have no idea *how* I can be that for her.

While they chat, I start to back away, and then slip back inside into the cabin. I quickly make my way through house and up the stairs, not stopping until I make it to my lookout room. I ignore the rifle leaned in the corner and go for the desk, pulling open the bottom left drawer. There sits a cell phone, and I pull it out along with its charger. I plug it in to charge, shoving it behind the desk, and then retreat, heading back outside with Gunner.

"Sorry, had to grab the dog," I say, clearing my throat when they both look at me. Gunner trots alongside of me, wagging his tail and then stopping to piss, playing the part exactly as he should.

"I'm sure Mr. Martin can give you the directions to the airport, if you'd like to meet your family," the officer continues to Emersyn, his voice bright. "From there, you can make your plan to either remain in the area or return home. I'll close the report. I highly suggest getting a phone, though."

"Thank you," she says with a soft smile, tears brimming her eyes. "I'll grab one as soon as I can."

I frown at the sight of her, still trying to adjust to *this* Em. I'm fucking flattered that she's not outing me for everything I've done, but I'm also unnerved by the ease in the way she's putting on a show.

The officer bids goodbye to the two of us, and then

climbs into his SUV, backing out of the driveway. Em lets out a heavy sigh, and then turns to me.

"You're coming with me, right?"

I raise my brows. "What?"

"To get a phone?"

"No, Em, I'm not. I'm not going with you anywhere." I spin on my heels and head back for the cabin. Now that the bubble has burst, and reality is crashing down around me, I know the answer to everything.

"Turner?" Em chases after me. "I'll come right back. I just need a phone to call my family and let them know I'm okay. I'm going to have to deal with Adam going missing..."

"I know," I say, holding the door open for her. "But even though I told you I'd work on things—I'd be good for you— that doesn't mean I can just go out gallivanting like a normal fucking person. I'm not fixed, Em."

Her lips part, brows furrowing. "I know that. I'm sorry. I'll go and take care of everything, and then I'll come back. Just let me get everything sorted... I'll stay with you. I'll get you a phone, too."

I close my eyes, turning to her. "I *have* a phone. I *have* access to the world. I *choose* not to use it."

Her jaw drops. "You told me you didn't."

"I lied."

She holds my gaze, hurt penetrating every inch of her face. "Okay. Well, it wouldn't have had service anyway." She slips past me, heading to the bedroom. As soon as she enters, she starts sifting through her bag, digging out her purse and wallet. "I'm going to make some coffee before I go." Em slings her purse across her body and then heads to the kitchen, leaving me there in the bedroom.

I can't handle this. I'll snap. I'll hurt someone. I'll hurt her in one way or another. The defeat hangs heavy on my shoulders. I know I told her I would be good, and maybe I *can* be good in a secure, controlled environment right now—but handling a hunt for a dead guy in my backyard? Meeting her family and trying to be normal? I'll never fucking make it. I'm not ready for that. I don't know how long it would take for me to *be* ready...

Or if I'd ever be ready.

I swallow the lump in my throat as I exit the room, the scent of coffee hitting me in the face. No matter how much I want Em, no matter how hard I promise to change, I *can't* be there for her.

And that's the ultimate sin.

CHAPTER 24

EMERSYN

MY HEART POUNDS in my chest as I take the last sip of my coffee. Turner has gone silent, leaning against the counter watching me. I don't care that he had a phone and didn't tell me. I don't care that he killed Adam. I don't care that he might be borderline insane with violent urges. I don't even care if I have to deliver warm bodies for him to fulfill his taste for violence.

I. Don't. Care.

"Thanks for being an alibi," Turner says quietly. "You didn't have to. You could've told him the entire truth, and I wouldn't have been mad at you."

Furrowing my brow, I set the mug down. "What did you want me to do? Turn you in? They'd put you in prison for the rest of your life, Turner."

He throws his hands up at me. "Have you *ever* considered that *maybe* that's where I belong? I mean, there's only so much someone could do, and I bet if Tommy knew—"

I swallow hard and cut him off. "I don't think he would change his mind."

"I'm a danger to society." He takes a step toward me. "There's no coming back from that."

"There is," I argue with him. "I know the police officer showing up was overwhelming, but it doesn't change what's happened between us. I don't feel any different about you."

"Fuck, Em," he grabs me, pulling me into his chest, and wrapping me up in a hug. He presses his lips to the top of my head. "Why are you such an angel, huh?"

"I'm really not," I laugh, tipping my head back to peer up at him.

He smiles, leaning down and taking my mouth with his. He kisses me, long and deep, taking his sweet time to canvas my mouth. I grip the back of his neck as he tightens his hands on my waist.

When we finally come up for air, he presses one last kiss to my forehead and then releases me. "You should probably get going. The last thing you want to do is raise some kind of suspicion now that your truck is out, and someone knows."

I hesitate. "Yeah, well, I just need to get a phone, and then I can come back. I had service when I was pulling up in the driveway."

"Yeah, you can get service in some places, but it's really spotty," Turner says carefully, eyeing me. "Hopefully, somewhere is open today."

"I'm sure there's somewhere that is," I reassure him, patting his chest. "I'll figure something out."

He rests his hand over mine, intertwining his fingers with

mine, before pulling it away from my chest. "You're a good person, Emersyn."

I nod slowly, my heart skipping a beat. "Yeah, well, I think that's actually debatable at this point, but thanks." I laugh it off and give Gunner a pat on the head as I make my way to the front door.

He chuckles, dropping my hand to open the front door for me. I step out, the sunshine glistening on the snow that hasn't been cleared. It's surreal seeing my truck parked about a hundred feet from the house, just inside of where the yard ends and the thick trees begin. My mind flashes back to the beginning—to when I first got stuck in the driveway.

I glance back at Turner, who closes the door behind us. Part of me wonders how such a small event, turning into the wrong drive, made such a massive alteration in my course of life. Did it do the same for him? Will it be enough to pull him from the pits of his mind's brokenness?

"You okay?" Turner furrows his brow.

"Yeah," I nod quickly, scrambling down the steps. "I was just thinking that I'll miss you while I'm gone." I know it's not the truth, but I *will* miss him when I'm gone, and I'll be worried about his wellbeing, too—even if it's just a trip to town to find a freaking phone and get the situation under control.

I walk out to my truck, and he follows, our boots crunching in the snow. He opens the driver's side door for me, and I kick the snow off my shoes on the running boards. I climb inside and grab for the keys, setting in the cupholder. I swipe them up and attempt to start it. It roars to life immediately, like it hasn't been buried in a blizzard for nearly two weeks. I open my mouth to say something, but Turner beats me to it.

"Go ahead and back down the drive. It shouldn't give you any trouble. I'll meet you down there."

"You can just ride with me?" I offer. "Or I can just say goodbye from here."

He leans in and kisses me, lingering in it for a few beats before pulling away. "Nah, I'll meet you down there, angel."

"Okay," I say, trying to read his cryptic expression. "Also—"

"See you in a minute," he cuts me off with a kiss on my nose. He steps away and shuts the door, and then waits for me to back up.

"Fine then." Huffing, I put the truck in reverse, and back down the driveway, navigating the cleared road. The tires never slip in four-wheel drive, and I suddenly wish he wouldn't have made it so easy to get out. Maybe then I could've stayed longer. However, I know he did it this morning, when he was initially planning on me to take Gunner and leave his body to rot.

And that thought leaves me nervous.

Surely, he won't do anything while I'm gone, right? I put the truck in park as I clear the gate, waiting for him. He said he'd meet me down here. I ignore the anxiety thrumming through my body as the minutes tick by. My hands begin to sweat, and as soon as I'm about to drive back up the driveway, I spot him, emerging through the trees.

He has a solemn expression, and before I realize exactly

what he's carrying, it's too late. He drops my bags at the front of my truck just as he slams the gate shut...

And locks it.

I fling open the truck door and race to the massive iron gate. "What are you doing, Turner?"

"You need to go," he says flatly. "For good."

"What?" My voice breaks, a sob choking it off. "What do you mean? I thought you said—"

"Em," he cuts me off, his voice sharp. "You *have* to go. You and I both know what happened here. You can call the cops, you can tell them the whole truth, and I won't hate you if they come get me. You can keep it to yourself and live with the burden of the truth, but it won't change my decision. I'm not well enough yet to go on the journey with you."

Tears stream down my cheeks. "You said you'd be good. I can... I can just..." I can't even get the words out as I reach through the steel pickets, desperate to reach him. "Turner, *please* don't make me do this alone."

"You're not alone. I'm giving you permission to do what's best for you, Em. Go take care of yourself."

"No," I break into a shout, fury mixing with the heartbreak. "No, I don't want to leave you alone. I don't want anything to happen to you."

He smiles. "I've made it almost forty-one years, and I'm still here. I just *can't* handle what comes next. We can't live in solitude while I try to figure out how to exist peacefully. There's too much going on. You *need* people who can be there for you, and that's not me."

"You selfish fucking coward," I scream at him, tears rolling down my cheeks as he stands just outside of my grip.

He shakes his head. "No, I'm not a coward. That's how I lived my life before you showed up here. Being a coward would be making you stay and try to navigate the shitstorm *and me*. You have to trust me, Em. This is what's best."

"No," I plead, gripping the cold steel and shaking it. "Just open the gate. Please just open the gate, Turner."

"I love you, Emersyn," he says, his voice painfully soft. "I have to do what I have to do, and you have to do the same for yourself." Turner takes a step forward, grabbing my hand and squeezing it. "Don't come back here."

"You'll get help though?" I choke out through the tears as his confession shakes me to my very core, followed by panic. "Right?"

"Yeah." He brings my hand to his lips, kissing my cold skin softly. "I promise. Good luck, Em. Do what's best for you. I'll never be mad either way." With that he drops my hand and steps away again. "Drive safe." He backs up, drifting closer to the tree line.

"I love you," I call out to him.

He closes his eyes and turns around, giving me his back instead of returning it. My heart rips in two as he disappears into the woods. I know I could come back. I know I could climb the fucking fence and sprint after him...

But what good would it do?

All I can hope is that somehow, Turner figures himself out. I force myself to take a deep breath, and scoop up my bags, throwing them in the backseat of my truck. I slam the door shut, and climb into the driver's seat, staring at the locked gate.

How will he find me if he wants to? Or does he not want to?

I purse my lips, sniffling as I flip open my console. I grab one of the blank Christmas cards from the box of cards I never sent. I pull it out, and scribble a note for him, leaving my phone number at the bottom. It's probably a waste, since I can assume he doesn't check his mail. However, I still shove it in the envelope, write his name on the front, and shove it in the black, rusted box just outside the gate.

I then climb back inside my truck, and I leave him.

Merry fucking Christmas, Turner.

CHAPTER 25

TURNER

I STARE DOWN at the phone in my hand, and then flick my gaze across the room to Gunner, who's sitting a few feet away. He's watching me carefully, as if somehow, he's been put in charge of ensuring I follow through. I run my tongue along my bottom lip. It would sure as shit be easier had I just went to the barn and done what I originally intended to do.

'Please get help.' I hear Em's voice in my head. It's been nearly a month since she left. I haven't paid any attention to the news, but no one has shown up here to search my property or arrest me. I haven't heard word on anything at all. It's as if everything just went right back to the way it was...

Everything but me.

I rake my hands over my face and set the phone down on the desk, standing to my feet. As I do, I peer out the window, spotting the mailman dropping by my mailbox. I might be detached from the world, but I swear I still get shitty junk mail like everyone else. I slip out of the room, Gunner hot on my heels. Thundering down the stairs, I head for the front door, stopping to slide on my boots and grab my parka.

"Come on," I instruct Gunner, heading out the front door. My heart thrums in my chest as I start down the driveway. There's been a couple more snows since she left, and if I had to guess, the search for her ex-boyfriend has been suspended until the thaw later this spring. I take a deep breath, shoving my hands in my pocket.

Maybe I should've tried to make things work with her. I frown at the thought. As much as I *want* that to have been a possibility, I know that it's not. I spent ten years living in a daze of violence... Two weeks with Em can't heal years of trauma. It doesn't work that way, and I'm not the kind of man who's going to pretend that it does. I need to reach out to someone who understands—and I haven't done it yet.

I'm letting you down, Em.

My boots crunch in the snow as I make it to the gate, I fish out the key, unlock it, and slip through. Gunner waits for me on the other side while I flip the lid open. I fish out a handful of envelopes, and then stand there sifting through it. It's all junk...

Until I reach the bottom envelope.

Turner is the only thing scrawled on it. I stare at it, my heart flipflopping in my chest. I glance around, wondering if *she* did it or if someone else drove out here. I rip it open to see a lame Christmas card. Sighing, I flip it open.

Turner,

I know you've made up your mind, and that's fine. I get it. I'd never expect you to jump back into society, and I'm sorry I made you feel that way. But I meant what I said. I love you, and I would've happily stood by your side through everything. I hope you find happiness, and if you ever change your mind...

I'll be here.

Love,

Em

There's a phone number scrawled at the bottom, and I zone out on the numbers for a few long moments, while my head tortures me with the flashbacks of her in my bed. It's hard enough living without her, and now my mind has shifted to reminding me of just how miserable that loss is. I shove the card in my pocket, and then slip back through the gate, shutting and locking it. I no longer dummy lock it anymore.

I *don't* want someone showing up here again.

I make the trek back to the house, stopping to dump the rest of the mail into the steel barrel I'll burn later. I then climb the porch steps and stomp the snow off the bottom of my boots. I cast my eyes out across the snowy woods, my chest aching as I take in desolation—the same that I found so much fucking comfort in for years. Now, I'm just reminded constantly that there's someone out there, outside of these walls, that *cares.*

Gunner lets out a whine at the door, breaking my thoughts. I spin on my heels and head inside for the evening, slipping off my shoes and locking the door behind me. I pull the card from my jacket as I hang it up on the rack, and head back up the stairs.

I glance down at her words again. *I'm so fucking sorry,*

Em. I wish I could be stable enough for you. I ascend the stairs back to the room, where the fully charged phone sits there, with four bars of service. I unlock it, and type in Em's number. My thumb hovers over the green *call* button, my heart in my ears.

I could just ask how she's doing now. See if she'd want to keep in touch by phone. But the knot in my stomach is the answer. It'd never be enough. I want to *be* there for her in the way she deserves.

I erase the number, but I don't set the phone down. Navigating to the contacts, I scroll to the one person who *might* still be willing to help me—and be able to handle me. Biting down on my bottom lip, I press the call button, hoping like hell he hasn't changed his phone number.

"Hello?" A deep, achingly familiar voice answers.

"Hey, I don't know... I don't know if you remember—"

"Martin," Bradford breathes out. "You really think I'd forget you?"

"Well, I guess not," I chuckle, fighting the way my chest is tightening. "I did try to hurt—"

"Water under the bridge," he cuts me off again. "I haven't heard from you in eleven years, Martin. How are you? Are you getting by?"

I swallow hard. "Uh, no. Not really. You ever get out?"

He chuckles. "Yeah, I got out a decade ago, kid. Where have you been?"

"The cabin," I answer him, flatly. "But I need to talk to you... I need some help."

He's silent for a few moments. "I'll be there tomorrow."

With that, the line goes dead, and I'm left with the phone still resting against my cheek in a stupor. I slowly pull it away, unsure if I did the right thing.

I set the phone down on the desk, and then wait.

———

GUNNER LETS out a bark at daybreak, and I peer through the window, spotting a black truck, pulling up outside of my gate. Pulse throbbing in my temple, I head out into the cold morning to the gate. I unlock it, as the driver's side door opens.

I'm staring my past right in the fucking face.

"You don't look well," Bradford comments, his gray eyes studying me beneath a black cowboy hat as he climbs out, leaving the gate between us. He's every bit as fit as ever, and even though he's got ten years on me, I wouldn't fight him. I've tried.

And I didn't win.

"You and I both know I haven't been well in years," I level with him, swinging the gate open. "But some things have happened, and I don't think I can keep going like this."

He purses his lips and blows out a sharp breath, the silver and black facial hair lining his jaw a new feature. "I don't know how you managed to keep this up for as long as you did. I've kept an eye on you."

"Not too close." My jaw ticks. "Otherwise, you'd probably have the cops with you."

"Nah, I don't want 'em around anymore than you do."

199

With that, he climbs back into his truck and pulls into my driveway. I close the gate, dummy locking it—just in case he needs to get out.

My hands sweat as I walk around to the passenger door, opening it and climbing inside. I stare down at my hands as we ride in silence to the cabin, where Gunner sits quietly on the front porch, watching us.

We exit then and I start to sweat even worse beneath my coat. I wipe my hands down my jeans, noticing Bradford watching me carefully. He stops on the front porch, giving Gunner a pat on the head before reaching into his denim sherpa pocket and pulling out a carton of cigarettes. He lights one up and holds out the box to me.

"I don't smoke anymore," I tell him, rocking back on my heels. I'm anticipating the urge for violence to wash over me at any moment, but it doesn't. All I can think about is Em— and if I'll be writing her a fucking letter from prison.

"With all the bodies you got buried around here, you probably should," Bradford chuckles. He takes a long draw and then puffs out a cloud of smoke. "Why didn't you call me after you killed Thomas?"

My head starts to feel light. "How do you know?"

He eyes me. "I told you, I've been keeping an eye on you, waiting for you to give me a call. I could use a guy like you. I can help you get healthy up here." He taps his temple. "You've been out playing risky behavior. You don't have to do that. I have contracts."

"I can't handle a real job."

"Good, I don't have a *real* job for you. I got a solution to

200

a longstanding problem you seem to have. It's up to you on whether or not you accept my help, but I can help you return to a new kind of normal—if that's what you want."

"I can't control the blackouts," I reason, unsure of what he means. "I only killed when someone showed up here... Or if I have a blackout."

"Yeah, I can help you with that. Give me the rest of the year to work with you, and I guarantee, you'll be good as new."

My heart jumps to my throat, thinking of Em. "Good enough to have a wife or some shit?"

Bradford laughs. "Sure. I got a few kids, too."

I take a deep breath. "I have no idea what this entails, but deal."

CHAPTER 26

EMERSYN

11 MONTHS LATER...

"Isn't this Christmas party amazing?" Catie's heels click obnoxiously as she prances up to me, a glass of champagne in her hands. Her hair is tied up in a perfectly fashioned half updo, and her small frame shows no sign of how much wine she drinks on the usual. "It's so much better to get drunk than it is to bake cookies and shit."

I blink a couple of times, taking in my drunk best friend in her tight red dress, low cut to nearly her belly button. "I suppose so." I turn my eyes back to the skyline of the city, and while it's not impressive, it's better than watching her.

"Can you believe they found all that data on Adam? I can't believe he was hiring prostitutes. God knows what he got himself into. He probably gave you the wrong address on purpose."

"Catie," I say in a sharp tone, the truth still stinging a little. For a man who called *me* a whore, he had been doing way more than I ever did. "I really don't want to talk about him tonight." My fingers brush across the wooden heart pendent resting against the black, long sleeve dress I'm wearing to this catastrophe of an elegant Christmas party.

A year. It's been a freaking year.

"Well, I'm still trying to cope with the fact that Aaron is in prison for doing the same fucking thing, Em. It's not like life is just a ball of fucking fun right now." Her voice drops, her shoulders dropping. "It's amazing what someone going missing does to their secrets. They all come out—whether we want them to or not."

I eye her, my faded paranoia tapping on my shoulder, but then nod. "I know. I'm sorry. You should get back to the party. Dustin, the guy you like from work, is here, you know. I saw him looking for you."

"Oh?" Her brows shoot skyward. "I didn't think he'd have the balls to come."

I shoot her a smile. "Well, I guess you were wrong."

"As per usual," she giggles. She then spins on her heels and clicks out of the sitting area, heading back where the bulk of the people are at around the bar. I continue to stand there, staring out into the night.

Fucking Christmas Eve.

My mind flashes back to that cabin in the woods, the one where I found myself, and then subsequently lost it. For a while, my mind told me debated on the truth with Adam and his hobbies, but as it turns out, it was legitimate—and Aaron was involved in the string as well.

I guess you never really know someone.

Tapping my nails on the side of my glass, I ignore the buzzing of my phone. It's more than likely my mom. Everyone is worried about me, but it's for all the wrong reasons. They see the way things played out with Adam, and they think I left my heart in Colorado. The truth is, I did. But it's at that stupid fucking cabin in the woods.

Fuck you, Turner.

I blink away the moisture that still somehow finds its way to my eyes, even after all this time has passed. I guess I don't move on as easy as I thought I did. I've considered going there so many times. I've thought about writing another letter, but I extended my offer when I stuck that Christmas card in his mailbox.

He has a phone, and he chose to never call. I take a deep breath and take a sip of my champagne. I don't know if I'm angry or bitter. I don't know if the infatuation with him morphed to hatred, or if I still love him. I don't *know*.

And that's the part I hate the most.

Catie says someday the heartbreak will fade, since she knows I fell for Turner. She doesn't know the rest. That's something I'll take to my grave without regret. My phone buzzes again, and I fish it out of my purse, flipping it open. I see the notification on social media, Catie tagging me in some godforsaken selfie with the bar we're at. We took a trip this year just for her.

"You really shouldn't let your friend tag you in posts that give away your location," a voice says from behind me with a deep chuckle. "It's dangerous, though helpful if someone wants to find you."

"Thanks for the advice," I mutter, still staring out the window. "Why don't you go talk to her about it?"

"I'd rather talk to you."

I feel the presence of the desperate guy, probably out to get laid, draw closer. "I'm not much for conversation. You're better off finding someone else." I wave him off, making it a point *not* to look. There's something familiar in the deep voice, and I know it's my mind playing tricks on me. It's happened before.

"That's funny, you never shut up when you were with me."

My pulse jumps in my throat, and I squeeze my eyes shut. *It can't be. It really can't be. It's impossible.*

"Em..."

My heart explodes in my chest as my eyes flutter open, and I finally peer up at the man standing a couple of feet from me. Turner stands there, holding a glass of champagne, and sporting a fucking *suit*. His hair is longer on the top and slicked back, ink scrawls up his neck and down his hands. His dark eyes are as intense as always, but...

They're filled fully with warmth.

"What are you doing here?" I manage to choke out, half tempted to pinch myself to make sure I didn't just drink a few too many. *I've only had one.*

"Well," he chuckles. "It took me a little longer than I thought it would, but this seemed as good of a time as any to catch up."

I shake my head at him, my knees feeling weak with emotion. "You never called."

"No, I didn't." He admits in a flat tone, downing the rest of his champagne and setting it on one of the small tables. "If I would've called, you wouldn't have stayed away—I wouldn't have stayed away. I had to have time to fix myself, Em. I followed through, but I had to do it on my time."

"Still, you broke my heart," I reason as he takes a step closer.

"Yeah, and I'm sorry, but it was better than accidentally killing you." He says the words with a confidence that's new and unnerving. "As it turns out, I was able to get everything I needed. Well, *almost*." He brushes his fingers down my arm.

But I don't budge, even as the familiar arousal pours through my body. "You can't just come back."

"I can." He gently grips my chin. "I know you still love me, Em. I've kept eyes on you the last few months, and you haven't moved on."

"You're making assumptions."

He chuckles. "Am I?"

I suck in a sharp breath at the woodsy scent filling my lungs. "So, you're just all better now? All ready to make it work now that I've gone through everything alone?"

A flash of remorse fills his expression. "You and I both know, it would've never worked out like that. I was in love with you, but I couldn't be what you needed. Sometimes," he brushes his nose against mine. "Sometimes, love *isn't* enough."

"You used the term *was*," I say, breathing out as I close my eyes, battling all the emotions and all the questions I want answers to.

He chuckles. "Yeah, *was*. Because I *was* in love with you, *and* I couldn't be what you need. Now, I'm *in* love with you, and I *can* be the guy you need. I can be here for you, Em." My eyes flutter open to meet his soft, dark irises. "I can go to your parties, meet your family, buy you the house with the picket fence, have the kids—you name it, angel, and I can give it to you. I just needed to take the first step myself."

I want to scream at him for all the heartbreak he caused me, but the sincerity in his voice nearly brings me to my knees. "What did you have to do?"

He threads his arm around my waist holding my body against his. "I had to reach out and get help from the person who had been offering it all along. It wasn't easy, Em, and the process of healing was dangerous. I was unstable, and I had to learn how to manage myself, and get the right treatment for my blackouts."

"And are they gone?" I whisper as he presses his lips to my jaw.

His hot breath against my ear sends a familiar shiver of arousal down my spine. "Yes, Em. But I'd be lying if I said they may never come back, but I can tell you that I'll never hurt you or myself ever again. I'm good."

I lean away from his intoxicating kiss. "Just like that, *you're good?*"

Turner chuckles. "Yeah, I'm *good*. I'm fucking *great* now that I've got my hands on you, and you know what, if you tell me I have to earn my keep for you, I'll do it. I'll fucking chase you for the rest of my life."

A smile tugs at my lips. "I'm not just letting you off the

hook, but..." My voice trails off as I take in *this* version of Turner. "I *do* understand that you needed time—and maybe help that I couldn't give you."

"I needed a solid risk assessment and space to become safe for you, Em," he replies, his voice dropping in volume. "I had to leave the cabin for a long time and work my way back. That's what I needed, and I never pursued it before because I didn't have a reason to. *You* were the reason I was waiting for."

"You became charming, I see," I swat a tear from under my eye. "You must have been practicing."

"I may have rehearsed a few lines," Turner murmurs, and then presses his lips to mine. I instantly melt into him, getting a new and old taste of him once more. His tongue slips between my lips, intertwining with my tongue. The same hunger is there, but there's a renewed sense of confidence that he didn't have before.

My champagne glass slips from my hand, spilling on the rug as we stumble back. "Turner," I break the kiss, giggling. "We're lucky that didn't break."

"Yeah," he chuckles, landing his lips on mine again for a light kiss before leaning away. "Does your friend have a ride home?"

"Yeah, her new guy," I answer him. "Why?"

"Because I'm fucking *dying* to get you home and out of this dress," he growls, dipping his hands lower, landing on my ass.

I peer up at him. "So, where is home now?"

He presses his forehead to mine. "Wherever you are."

Epilogue

Turner

Two years later...

"Em," I call out as I grab my jacket and head downstairs. "Do you know where my phone is? Bradford will be here at any time."

"It's probably lost in the couch again," she laughs as I enter the kitchen, now adorned with pictures of us—and my family intermixed. It still hurts sometimes, but it doesn't trigger me. I take in the sight of Em, and smile. She's in a pair of light wash jeans and a hideous Christmas sweater, but even so, she looks as beautiful as ever.

And the best thing we ever did was remodel this damn cabin.

New floors, new paint, new kitchen, and well, there's a lot of gawdy cabin décor that she loves. But I let it happen.

"I swear I always lose my phone," I mutter under my breath as I plant a kiss on her cheek and run my hand across her stomach. *Four months to go.* "This job shouldn't take long."

"I know," she chimes, glancing back at me as I slip into the living room. "Is Gunner going?"

"No, he can stay with you," I answer her, eyeing my elderly dog. He's pushing up there now, and I don't know how he's made it this long, but he has—and I hope he makes it to the birth of my first kid.

But the puppy might push him over the edge.

I frown at the little ball of energy mutt bouncing on top of him, and then rolling around on the hardwood floor. "Why did we think a puppy was a good idea?" I think aloud, glancing back to Em, who turns around to face me.

"Um, because you'll need him. You're not invincible, Turner," she reminds me, just like always, though it's with a smile.

"Right, he just looks like he's going to be a shithead," I laugh as the puppy, who she named Boomer, runs up and starts playing tug of war with my jeans.

"Well then the two of you should get along just fine," Em bursts into a fit of giggles as I shoot her a dirty look. The sun shines through the front windows, no longer covered by curtains, and the hint of light glints off her wedding ring.

We somehow managed to make the move back to this cabin, even with all the secrets buried around the place. But it's different now. The air isn't heavy, and the days aren't dark. We laugh, and my job and medication keep the urges away. Bradford taught me methods to control myself, and my job of hunting people down... Well...

It's good for the fucked up person inside of me.

"Who is it this time?" Em asks, drawing me out of my thoughts.

"No idea. He just said it was someone who deserted and is on the run in the foothills. I'm sure it won't take long. It never does."

She nods. "True. You're efficient."

"And you're fucking hot," I breathe out as I take in her full lips, and her disheveled brown hair on top of her head. "I hate leaving you on Christmas."

Em laughs, grabbing my shirt and tugging me into her. "We already celebrated, but..." She stands on her tiptoes and kisses my jaw. "It just means you owe me later."

I run my tongue along my bottom lip. "I do, huh? I could probably make a little time to make good on that right now."

"Oh please," she swats my chest. "How about let's *not* get caught by Bradford. I'd want to crawl into a hole and die."

"Damn, that's intense. I didn't know it was so embarrassing to be with me." I shoot her a wink and then sigh. "I really do hate taking off on this day though."

"Yeah, I know," her voice grows soft. "But this isn't an easy day, and it's better spent in the field."

I eye the wooden pendent, still hanging around her neck. "Not everything about this day is all that bad," I tell her, reaching out and brushing my fingers across the heart. "Sometimes, the best and worst days can be interchangeable." I meet her gaze. "He'd be glad that we're turning his room into a nursery, you know."

She brushes her hand across my cheek. "Yeah, I bet he would, and if it's my guess, I bet he'd be really proud of you."

"Maybe," I say, emotions swelling in my chest as I kiss her on the forehead. The sound of an engine grows outside the cabin and I sigh. "I have a feeling my brother would want to smack me across the face for a few things as well."

"Meh, details." She places a kiss on my lips. "You better get going. I'll see you when you get home."

"Keep the gate locked and the fire going," I tell her, running my thumb along her bottom lip. "You know I hate leaving you."

"And I know you'll always come back to me." She gives me a look. "Besides, Catie is coming over. She's got herself another new boyfriend."

"Lovely," I mutter, kissing her once more. "I love you, Em."

"I love you, too."

I give Gunner and Boomer a good pat, and then slip out the front door. Bradford's truck waits just outside, and he honks the horn a couple of times. I flip him off and grab my duffle bag from where it sits on the front porch. I toss it into the back of the truck, taking one last look at Em and Gunner, watching me through the window.

She blows me a kiss, and I wink at her once more. I got fucking lucky when it comes to her, and that's something I'll never stop thanking the universe for. I whip open the passenger door and climb in.

"Merry Christmas, asshole," I tell Bradford, smacking his arm as he lights up a cigarette. "You really should quit that."

"Yeah, okay, Mom," he shoots back at me with a grin. "But Merry Christmas to you, too. I was hoping we could take the holidays off, but duty calls."

I nod, a rush of excitement flooding through my veins as he backs out of the driveway. "So a deserter, huh?"

"That's all I've got. He's apparently violent as fuck, walks around wanting to pick a fight." Bradford puffs on his cigarette as he puts the truck in park, waiting for me to shut the gate. I slide out, shut and lock it, and then climb back in.

"What's the goal with him?" I ask as he tears down the road, heading north. "You want to take him out or recruit him?"

Bradford shrugs. "We'll feel him out when we get there. Not everyone is cut out to come and work for me. Being a mercenary is a bit of a calling, I'd say. It's not for the weak minded, don't you think?"

I lean back in the seat, clicking the belt in place. "I don't know. I thought I was pretty weak minded. It took me a long time to figure out I just needed a different mental outlook."

"Yeah, you needed an ass kicking is what you needed, Martin," he snorts. "And I have to admit it felt good to be the one to give it to you."

I chuckle, gazing out the window at the snow-covered ground. "I suppose I deserved that."

"Meh, water under the bridge, as I always say," Bradford grins, rolling down the window enough to suck the smoke from the cab. The diesel engine roars as he stomps the gas, flooding the road behind us with a puff of black coal. "I always hoped you'd call."

"Just ten years late," I laugh, tipping my head back. "Sorry about that."

"Nah, it's never too late. You had to find your reason. You didn't have it until Em. She's a catch."

"I know," I agree, smiling to myself as I think back to my wife, staying cozy and warm in the cabin. "Hopefully, this'll be a quick one."

"It's always quick when you're behind the gun, Trigger."

"Yep." I lean my head back, closing my eyes and taking a few deep breaths as I run through my mental checklist. My rifle is tucked away safely in my duffle bag, freshly cleaned, and ready to go on another mission. All the rest of my gear never leaves the bag. My hands sweat with anticipation, and I grin to myself.

As it turns out, I get to have my cake and eat it, too. I get the girl, the picket fence, *and* the fun.

I just had to be taught how to make friends with my monster.

Also by ANNIE WILD

No Control: A Dark Romance

Killing Emma: A Dark Captive Romance

The Huntress and Her Hound: A Dark Serial Killer Romance

Run & Hide: A Dark Halloween Romance

About the Author

I love creating slow burn, dark, suspenseful, and broody romances that question just how far into the gray we're willing to go for love.

When I'm not creating morally gray men and writing their redemptive arcs, you can find me going for hikes in the woods with my four dogs or immersing myself in a true crime podcast

Made in the USA
Las Vegas, NV
01 December 2024

13011934R00132